At breakfast Mama said she didn't feel like sight-seeing. "You go on and take Bizou," she said to Nicholas, the guy we met on the plane. She said she still felt tired and would just be a drag on us.

We had a good day. Nicholas took me up to Columbia University where he went to college and met Tara, a girl he's not sure likes him any more. Mama had said she'd meet us at the Statue of Liberty at four so that's where we ended up. Four-thirty came and still Mama hadn't showed. She can do that. She doesn't like wearing a watch.

Finally we just went back to the hotel. The man at the desk took Nicholas aside and said something to him. He gave him a letter. Then he came over to me and said there was one for me too. I don't know why I started feeling scared. Here's what my letter said:

═══════════════════════════

Dear Bizou,

Honey, I just feel like I've got to get off by myself for a while. You stay with Nicholas and be good, and I'll get in touch with you sometime soon.

Tranquility

Other Fawcett Books
by Norma Klein:

BEGINNERS' LOVE

IT'S OKAY IF YOU DON'T LOVE ME

LOVE IS ONE OF THE CHOICES

THE QUEEN OF THE WHAT IFS

COMING TO LIFE

DOMESTIC ARRANGEMENTS

LOVE & OTHER EUPHEMISMS

NORMA KLEIN
BIZOU

FAWCETT JUNIPER • NEW YORK

RLI: $\dfrac{\text{VL: 4 + up}}{\text{IL: 8 + up}}$

A Fawcett Juniper Book
Published by Ballantine Books

Copyright © 1983 by Norma Klein

All rights reserved under International and Pan-American Copyright
Conventions. Published in the United States by Ballantine Books, a
division of Random House, Inc., New York, and simultaneously in Canada
by Random House of Canada Limited, Toronto.

Library of Congress Catalog Card Number: 83-6932

ISBN 0-449-70109-3

This edition published by arrangement with The Viking Press

Manufactured in the United States of America

First Ballantine Books Edition: October 1985

To Merrill Joan Gerber

Chapter 1

"**D**oesn't your mother want any dinner, dear?" The stewardess was looking over at Mama, who was out cold, leaning on her cheek, breathing quietly.

"I guess she might want some later," I said. But it got me mad. Here Mama said she had to have the window seat, even though it was *my* first airplane ride and she's been in planes hundreds, maybe thousands of times, and then she konks out practically before we're in the air. I know why, too. It's two things. One, she gets nervous from flying and she thinks being in the window seat brings good luck. Also she says if she can see what's going on outside the plane, she feels better. Of course if she's asleep, how can she see anything? It was nighttime, anyway. The other thing is she gets airsick, so she takes all these little green pills that make you real sleepy. I told her I wouldn't take

1

one. I'd rather get sick, throw up, and then be really awake.

The stewardess unfolded our trays and asked me what I thought Mama would like. There was a choice: chicken made some fancy way or beef. Mama's like me, she's crazy about chicken, so I checked that for both of us. If she doesn't wake up till after they serve, I'll save her roll and cake for later.

Next to me, on my other side from Mama, was a man. About twenty, maybe. He told the stewardess he didn't want chicken *or* beef, said he was a vegetarian. "Well, I'll see what I can do about that," she said in a kind of snippy way. She looked mad. I bet anything she brings him a big bowl of lettuce and some cheese. That's one reason I'd never be a vegetarian, though I can see it from the point of view of loving animals. If I lived on a farm and had to really kill them to eat, I guess I'd go off meat and chicken too, maybe.

After the stewardess went away, the man said, looking over at Mama with a worried expression, "Is she okay?"

"Sure." I told him about Mama taking all those pills for motion sickness.

"You have to be careful with those," he said. "They can be dangerous."

He must've meant taking too many by mistake. I said, "Don't worry. She knows how many to take."

Mama's kind of a pill freak. She takes lots of stuff. She says she knows what she's doing and lots of the pills are just vitamins to keep up her strength because she's always been a little too skinny, like me. She makes me take vitamins, too: four every morning, real big ones. If I wasn't real good at swallowing pills, I'd be in trouble because these pills are huge—like

2

jellybeans, almost. She says it's because her father was a doctor and she grew up knowing lots about nutrition.

You want to know something strange? That's all I know about Mama's family: that her father was a doctor and she grew up in a college town somewhere. I don't even know where, what state or anything. She won't even tell me her maiden name. I've got some theories about it, but it's something she just won't talk about. See, what I think is this. I think Mama's family got mad at her for some reason, and so she left home. She came over to Paris when she was eighteen to be a model and she never did go back. This is my first trip to the United States, and I'm thirteen already. Of course, we studied all about America in school, and I've seen lots of American movies. I know a lot, but just that way, from books and movies, not from really seeing, which, in my opinion, is the best way to know about something. One thing I do know from Mama, and this is why she decided to raise me in Paris. She says people in the United States treat black people bad. She says maybe it's better in some parts, but it's still not all that good, and she didn't want me growing up in a country that was crazy in that particular way. She says the French are crazy in lots of other ways, but not as far as color goes. That's true. Nobody ever said anything mean to me just on account of the way I look, and I can tell you if anyone starts that over there, they better look out.

Mama's family probably got even madder at her for marrying my father, who was white. He was French and a journalist. I'm not saying he was famous, like John Lennon or something, but he was really well-known, and he covered stories all over the world.

That's how he was killed when I was three. He was in Vietnam on a story, and some fighting started, and he couldn't hide fast enough. They gave him a medal after he died, and they printed up this big book of all his best photos. It's a truly great book. I showed it to my teacher this year. She said I must be really proud of him, and I said yes, I was. I think if Mama's family had ever met my father, maybe they'd have changed their mind. But I don't think they ever did.

Mama just won't talk about it! All this that I've been saying I've kind of picked up and pieced together, but if I ask her directly, she looks kind of stony and says she won't talk about it. So why are we going back all of a sudden now when all along she's said how she hates America and her family? I don't exactly know. Mama just said it was time I saw America. She said she had some good friends she still felt kindly toward. Maybe she was influenced by this TV show "Roots" they had on last year. She made me sit down and watch all of it, which for Mama is rare, let me tell you. She doesn't like me watching TV much. But she said the point was that knowing what your roots are is important and maybe she'd made a mistake telling me so little. She said that, but she didn't say much *after* that. So I guess taking me is a way of showing.

Mama was still sleeping when the stewardess brought our food. I looked over at the man's plate. All they gave him was a big salad. "You can have my roll," I said.

"You sure?"

"Yeah, you can have Mama's roll too."

He hesitated a minute. Then he took them both and

said, "Thanks. Hey, I'm Nicholas, by the way, or Nick, whatever you prefer. What's your name?"

I told him, "Eliane." You have to pronounce that "El Yan." Some American kids in the school I go to say "Elly Anne."

"Eliane," he repeated. He got it right. "Are you French?"

"Half," I said. I told him about Mama and how she'd never been back in fifteen years and about how she said there was so much prejudice.

He frowned. "I guess she's probably right," he said. "I'm from New York, and maybe it's less extreme there. My best friend in high school was black, but that might not be typical."

"What grade are you in now?" I asked him. I'm not so good at figuring people's ages. He looked like almost twenty, but maybe younger. He had a lot of freckles and a round face.

He laughed. Then he told me how he was twenty-three. He graduated from college last year, and he decided to take a year off, to travel around France, playing guitar and taking it easy. Now he has to go back and go to medical school to be a doctor. "I'm not looking forward to it," he said. He wasn't eating much of his salad, just shoving it around kind of, but he ate all three rolls, ours and his. Mama would say that wasn't a well-balanced meal.

"Don't you want to be a doctor?" I said.

"No way. I hate doctors."

"So why're you doing it?"

"I'm a coward." He grinned. "No, seriously, my grandparents paid for this trip, this year, if I promised to go through med school, so I figure it would be kind of chicken to back out. And then you've got to earn a living. . . . You know what I'll do? I'll be a doctor, I'll make lots of money, then I'll spend half of each year doing what I want—music, painting, lazing around."

"That's what Mama does," I told him. "I mean Tranquility." If I call Mama "Mama" in public, it makes me sound babyish, so I'm trying to break the habit. But Tranquility's such a weird name, I hate to say *that* either. "She's a model, but the rest of the time she studies and learns a lot about different things. She never went to college, but she knows more now than most people who did."

"What does she study?"

"Everything! Archaeology, French poetry, Eskimos . . ."

"And she finances it all by modeling?"

"Yeah." I saw him look over at her again. One look at Mama and you know: she has style. She's told me about this lots of times, and I can tell as soon as I look at a lady whether she has it or not. It's not looks, though Mama is pretty. She's real tall and dark and she has big, big black eyes. She always wears her hair the same way: straight back with big dangling earrings. Some ladies look severe that way, but Mama looks sharp and neat. And she always wears white or red; those are her favorite colors. Right now she was wearing a white pantsuit, and even sleeping, with her mouth open a little, she looked good.

"You look like you could model too," Nicholas said. "Have you ever thought of it?"

I wrinkled my nose. "I don't want to. . . . And Tranquility doesn't want me to either. She says you get to trade off too much on your looks that way. And she

6

says half the models she knows are real basket cases, on drugs and stuff. She wants me to use my head."

"I know what you mean," Nicholas said. "I dated a girl once who was a model, and she was a real airhead . . . That means someone who's not too well-stocked up here," he explained, tapping his head.

"I know," I said. Even though I've always lived in France, I go to a bilingual school where lots of the kids are American, so I know all those expressions. Peter, my boyfriend from the first part of the year, was American. He was in my school two years. Then all of a sudden his father was transferred back to the U.S.

"You seem to know a lot," Nicholas said.

"I do," I told him, "for thirteen." It's true. I wasn't just boasting. Mama says maybe I grew up too fast, the two of us alone and all, but I like it. There's no point in being backward in today's world. That's another thing Mama believes. Me too.

Chapter 2

Mama just kept straight on sleeping. It was night after a while. I knew I should've felt sleepy, but I didn't. I started thinking about Peter and whether we'd have a chance to see him once we were over there. I know Mama has plans of her own, but maybe if we're in Washington, D.C., which is where he lives, we can stop off. I have his address and his phone number. He said if I ever made it over there, I should call. The trouble is, maybe by now he has another girl friend. It's only been six months, but Mama says some men move fast.

I feel bad about one thing. The whole time Peter was in my school, I liked him, but I also liked Jean-Claude, and I kept trying to figure out who I liked best. It was like I liked them both in different ways. Jean-Claude is someone I've known since I was eight, when I switched to the American School. He's French, but his mother's American. The thing is, he's really funny-looking. When I first saw him, I just started to laugh, which I know is rude, but I couldn't help it. He has a big nose and black eyes and a big funny smile, almost from ear to ear, and black hair that hangs right into his face. And he's always horsing around, telling jokes. He's fun to be with, almost more like a girl friend except he started liking me the other way at the beginning of seventh grade, this year, and I began liking him.

Peter's good-looking. Mama says that's a bad thing. She says women can be good-looking and not be vain, but men never. "Look out for men who are too good-looking." I don't know. I don't think Peter is vain. He's brown-skinned, like me, and has dark eyes and a great smile. And he's a *really* good kisser.

I thought maybe once Peter left, it would be easier. I'd just like Jean-Claude. But it wasn't. I can still start liking someone for no really good reason, and then the next day I'll like someone else. I hope I'm not going to be fickle. Mama says fickle women drive men crazy, and I don't want to do *that*. But I sure don't want to marry at nineteen, like she did. She says she didn't either, but she met my father and that was that.

Nicholas fell asleep after a while, but I never did. I sat there, thinking about everything, feeling excited about what lay ahead. I didn't feel nervous, not at being in an airplane, not even at going someplace I never was before. About an hour before we were due to land, Mama woke up. She stretched and yawned and looked over at me.

"We're almost there," I told her. I showed her the cake I'd saved for her, but she said she was more thirsty and asked the stewardess for some orange

9

juice. "You slept the whole time," I told her. "You didn't even *need* the window seat."

"Are you still bearing a grudge about that?" Mama said, smiling. "It's dark anyway. There's nothing to see."

It was eleven at night New York time, five o'clock in the morning French time. I don't know why I wasn't sleepy, because it was the middle of the night! "I gave him our rolls," I said, explaining about how Nicholas was a vegetarian and got stuck with just lettuce for dinner.

Then Nicholas woke up, and I introduced him to Mama. "I hope Eliane didn't bother you talking too much," she said.

I was so relieved she called me "Eliane" I almost forgot to get mad at her saying that. When we're alone Mama always calls me "Bizou," from when I was a baby. It sounds like bee-zoo, and it means "little kiss." I guess it's a cute baby name, but how would *you* liked to be called Bizou at thirteen? She says my father thought it up because I always wanted to give him one more little kiss before I went to sleep.

"We had a good talk," Nicholas said. "She's really mature for her age."

"Too mature," Mama shot back.

"Kids are like that today," he said.

Boy, I hate it when grown-ups talk like you're not there! "He plays the guitar," I told Mama.

"Oh, my husband played the guitar," Mama said. One habit I can't break Mama of: she always talks about my father, practically like he was still alive. She says that's because she still thinks of him a lot, and if he's alive in her mind, he's alive, period. Don't think that means she hasn't had any boyfriends since he died. She has, and even thought of marrying some of them. But in the end she'd always say they didn't measure up to my father. She doesn't want to settle down. She's willing to live alone for the rest of her life rather than that, she says.

Mama's a true independent woman, and she says men don't always like that. Or they like it, but when they get close, they want to kind of take over, show her how to do things, help her out. And she says, "No, thanks. I can do that myself." She doesn't mind if they want to share, but she can't abide men who take over. I'm like that too. I don't like boys that try to put me down in any way, and believe me, they try. Like teasing you if you're not good at something. Or acting like if you weren't pretty, they wouldn't seek out your company. I say if all they want is pretty, let them find some other girl, not me!

By the time the plane landed and we had to wait to get through customs, I was almost dead asleep. That's what comes from not sleeping on the plane. I looked around, trying to see if people looked different, but I couldn't tell. It was just that all the signs and everything were in English. But the people looked pretty much the same.

"I don't know if I can make it into the city," Mama said when we were through customs. "I'm beat."

"You slept, Mama," I reminded her.

"I know, but I'm beat anyway."

"There's a hotel near the airport," Nicholas said. "I'm staying there. Why don't we share a cab?"

He had more bags than us, but the driver got us all loaded up and we drove off.

We must've done all that stuff of checking into the hotel and setting up in our room, but to tell the truth, I don't remember any of it. I must've been asleep standing on my feet. Mama said she used to get that way when she was in some opening and she'd been rehearsing around the clock and the designer was going so crazy, changing things at the last minute, that he wouldn't even let the models go home to rest. She says she learned from that how to work on automatic pilot, which means you just keep going and try to look like you know what you're doing no matter how foggy or strange you feel in your head.

When I woke up, I got scared. I couldn't remember where I was! I looked around the room. At first I thought I was with Mama on one of her jobs. Usually she doesn't take me, she has me stay over with a friend so I won't miss school, but occasionally she takes me along. I went to Calcutta, India, with her once. That was a downer. There were kids my age begging in the streets. And we've stayed in real fancy rich countries with practically nothing but beach and people lying under umbrellas. According to Mama even in those countries someone's doing the work, whether there are real beggars or not.

I looked more around the room. Where was Mama? We double up if we share a room sometimes, but she wasn't in the bed. For a second I wondered if she and Nicholas had gone off together, just for that one night. Don't get the wrong idea about Mama—she's not a one-night stander. But she says sometimes she'll meet a cute guy and get the urge, even if she doesn't especially want to be lifelong friends with him. She says that's okay, as long as you know what you're doing and don't expect more than what you're likely to get. But Nicholas didn't seem so much her type. Mama claims she doesn't have any special type so much. As long as they've got something to offer, she says they can come in any shape, size, or age they want. Like my father was fifteen years older than her, but that doesn't mean she's hung up on older men. That's true. Pierre, who lived with us a year almost, was five years younger than Mama. She says with men, like with everything, you've got to keep an open mind.

But I still didn't think Mama would've done that on our first night here, mainly because she's been acting so worried about it. Do you believe this? She packed and unpacked five *times* in the last two weeks, saying we're going, we're not going. Finally I sat down and said *I* wouldn't unpack one more time, and that was it.

I went to the bathroom. On the mirror I saw a note Scotch-taped on in Mama's handwriting. It said: "8 a.m.: Having breakfast with Nicholas in the coffee shop downstairs. Come on down when you're hungry, hon."

That got me going fast. I know I should've stopped to shower and freshen up. Mama likes me to every day, now that I'm almost a teenager. She says you start getting body smells, which aren't so bad, but you've still got to watch it. I know! One day I stayed at Yvonne's house, and we didn't wash all weekend. We both stunk. I couldn't stand to go near *her*, and she couldn't stand to go near *me*. It wasn't our fault, though. The hot water pipe burst in her building.

When I went downstairs, I saw Mama and Nicholas having breakfast. It was strange, all the plates of food on the table. At home Mama has coffee with milk and maybe a roll if she's hungry. "These are pancakes," Mama said. "You try some, Beez."

Peter's mother made pancakes once, so I know what

13

they're like. They're like crepes, only fatter, and you put something sweet on them, like jam or honey. I slid in next to Mama. "When did you wake up?" I asked her.

She laughed. "Never went to sleep—can you imagine? Nicholas and I just stayed up talking. I felt too nervous to close my eyes."

"Were you too nervous too?" I asked Nicholas.

"I can get by with very little sleep," he said. "Four hours, five."

"Oh, I love sleep," Mama said, stretching. "But sometimes, for months even, I just don't sleep! What can you do? . . . How about you, hon? Were you okay?"

"I don't even remember checking in," I admitted.

"You were out cold. Nicholas carried you. What am I going to do when she hits ninety pounds?" she asked him.

I'm five feet tall, and I weigh eighty-six, but I'm planning on growing. My father was six feet two and Mama's five nine, so something strange would have to happen for me to be a shrimp forever. Little bitty women get talked down to by men, and I wouldn't care for that at all, let me tell you.

"Nicholas said he'd show us around today," Mama said. "He went to college in New York, so he knows all the spots, not just touristy places."

"I thought *you* lived in New York once," I said to her.

"Just for six months," she said, "and that was fifteen years ago. I guess things've changed since then."

"I've been away a year," Nicholas said. "It's going to take me a while to readjust, I think."

"Would you have stayed in France?" I asked him. I'd had all the pancakes I could stomach for one morning.

"Oh, sure!" he said. "I love France, I love the people, everything."

"Live and let live," Mama said. "That's what I like about the French. They're as crazy as Americans, but they believe in letting people do their own thing."

Just then the waitress came over. She looked from me to Nicholas to Mom. She was wearing a blue uniform with a tag on it: Miss Rhonda. "Are you finished?" she said, starting to take our plates away.

"We'd like to sit and talk a while longer," Nicholas said, "if that's all right with you."

"No, it's not all right," the waitress said. "You've been sitting here two hours already. You better move on."

"My daughter just woke up," Mama said.

"Those are the rules," this Miss Rhonda said.

"What rules?" said Nicholas, looking mad.

"You can't just sit and sit. We need room for other customers."

Nicholas looked around the room. There were about ten empty tables. "Looks like you've got plenty of extra room," he said.

"I didn't make the rules!" the waitress said, slapping down the check. "Want to speak to the manager?"

Nicholas started to say something, but Mama put a hand on his. "We had enough to eat," she said quickly. "Let's go."

Outside the restaurant Mama flared up. "That's what I mean! Things *haven't* changed. We should've stayed home."

15

"What do you mean, Mama?" I asked.

"That lady thought we were a family and she didn't like it," Mama said.

"How can you tell?" I asked her.

"I can tell!" Mama snapped. To Nicholas she added, "My husband and I came over here on our honeymoon, and we had that scene re-enacted ten dozen times. Do I care who that lady is with? That Miss Rhonda? Do I care what *her* personal life is, *if* she has one?"

"Why didn't you let me speak to her?" Nicholas said.

"I hate scenes," Mama said. "Let ignorant people drown in their own ignorance."

I felt bad, wondering if Mama was right. She can blaze up real fast sometimes and then cool down. But I could tell our trip had gotten off to a bad start.

Chapter 3

We left our stuff at the hotel, planning to return there to sleep that night. Nicholas took us around New York. He took us to the top of the Empire State Building. I was glad, even though Mama called it touristy. No matter what Mama says, I was excited to be there. I could even call Peter up tonight if I felt like it! I'd have to find out first how much it cost. He'd be really surprised, I bet.

Maybe because I was thinking about him, I saw this boy I thought *was* him. He was looking through a telescope to see the view. When I came over and started to say something, he looked up, and I saw he didn't look like Peter that much—he was just the same height and color. "I thought you were someone I knew," I explained.

He grinned. "Maybe I am."

I knew he wasn't, but he was kind of cute, so I said, "Is your name Peter?"

"Nope. Is that the only name you like?"

"What's your name?"

"Spark."

"That's your real name?"

"Yeah . . . because I have a short fuse."

Just then I heard Mama yell, "Bizou."

I smiled at him. " 'Bye," I said.

"Hey, wait a sec," he said. "You live in New York?"

"Paris."

He looked like I had said something weird. "Paris, France?"

I nodded. "Nice to meet you," I said in French.

But when I got up to Mama, she looked really mad. "Who was that boy?" she demanded.

"His name's Spark," I told her.

"Listen," she said. "Do you want to get in trouble your first day in this country?"

"Why's it trouble to talk to somebody?" I said.

"If you start fooling around with strange boys, you're going to be in trouble fast!"

"Mama, I wasn't fooling around!" Here she says she loves flirting and it's a fine art and you've got to learn through practicing. "I was just flirting."

"You leave that for when we're back home. Americans don't understand flirting. They think everything is a pickup, has to lead to action."

Nicholas laughed. I felt embarrassed to have him hear Mama chewing me out like I was a baby who didn't know how to do things. "Did you ever pick a girl up?" I asked.

"Sure."

"See!" I said to Mama. "He didn't get into any trouble. . . . Did you?"

Nicholas shook his head. Then he and Mama said together, "It's different for girls."

"How's it different?" Half the time Mama tells me there's no difference, that women have to act just like men only more so to get ahead. Talk about inconsistent!

"Men rape and murder women," Mama said. "Women don't rape and murder men."

"Okay, okay," I said. I didn't want any lecture. I *know* all that!

They should've named *her* Spark. She can sure have a short fuse at times.

The rest of that whole day Mama was in a bad, bad mood. She has different bad moods. Sometimes she's like that, sparky and jumping all over you for nothing. The other kind is when she's quiet and just stares off into space. I hate that second kind of mood the worst because you don't know where you are *or* where she is. Nicholas took us to different places—Central Park, Grant's Tomb, Times Square. Wherever we went, Mama had something bad to say. Times Square was the worst. "Look at this dirt," she said. "*Look* at this!"

It's true, there was a lot of stuff just in the street— papers, everything. And it smelled. Maybe some cities smell worse than others. Or maybe it was that it was a hot day. Some of the smells were good—sweet smells like candy. Some were bad, like someone had peed right there on the sidewalk. But it was interesting. I was having a good time, even if Mama wasn't.

We stopped in a penny arcade to play some

electronic games. Peter had told me about those. I did Pac-Man and Tempest. I was pretty good after I got the hang of it. Nicholas watched me, but Mama just stood to one side, looking haughtily, her hip stuck out the way she sometimes stands. Then we had a bad scene, maybe the one that turned Mama off New York or America most of all. I heard it because, even though I was playing the game, Mama was only three feet away from me.

Two men, older than Nicholas, came up to Mama. They said, "Hi, honey!"

She didn't say anything.

"We're new in town," one of them said. "We don't know where to go or what to do."

Mama still didn't say anything.

"Maybe you'd like to help us out, okay? We got a lot of cash on us. We like pretty girls, no matter what color they are." I guess one of them reached out to touch Mama or show her his money. Anyway, she gave a yell and said, "Get your filthy hands off me, you pig!" When Mama yells, sometimes she gets a French accent.

That got the men real mad. One of them grabbed Mama and said, "Who're you calling a pig, you black bitch!"

I marched over and stood right in front of her. "You leave her alone!" I said. "That's my mother!"

The man grinned at his friend. "Hey, she's kind of cute. Want to double-date, honey?"

I couldn't think of any bad words to call him in English, so I called him a whole bunch in French. He looked at me like I was crazy. Then Nicholas came over and shoved the man aside.

"Cut it out," he said.

"Oh, boy, they've got a sucker already," the other man said.

"Move on," Nicholas said. "I mean it." You could tell he was kind of scared.

"Let's go," Mama said nervously. "Please." She grabbed Nicholas by one arm and me by the other. We jumped into a cab that came by. In the cab Mama started to cry.

Nicholas said, "Christ, I'm sorry."

"Those were ugly men," I said.

"Times Square's an ugly *place*," Nicholas said. "Listen, I'm really sorry. I should've thought."

"I want to go home and take a nap," Mama said in a far-off voice.

I put my hand on her shoulder. "Are you okay?"

"Yeah, I'm okay," Mama said, but she sounded real out of it. "I just want to sleep for around a hundred years and wake up and find the world's a different place."

No one said much on the way back in the cab. Now that it was over, I felt scared, thinking back on those men and how, maybe, they could've just killed us. In parts of America people still carry guns. I'm glad we weren't in one of those places.

At the hotel we said we'd meet Nicholas for supper and went to our room. Mama went straight to bed. I didn't know *what* to do. I thought of calling Peter, but then I was afraid I'd wake Mama up. Maybe when she wakes up, she'll decide we have to go back to Paris. But bad things can happen *any* place, not just America.

I took a really long hot bath. There was soap

wrapped up in paper and lots of towels stacked in one corner.

One thing I can't get used to yet is having a figure, by which I mean breasts. I only turned thirteen three months ago, and the funny thing is I can't remember now *when* I started to get them. I know I came to school in the fall and the first thing I noticed was that Yvonne had grown some over the summer. I kidded her a whole lot, which now seems ironical since little did I know I'd be getting them myself that soon. I sort of thought they'd come with my period, which I haven't gotten yet, but Mama says no, either one can come first. One thing I truly hope and pray is that I don't have big breasts. Mama doesn't. Hers are small and high up and she says that's the best kind of figure for clothes. She says if you have real big ones, they sag and hang down and men can't seem to notice anything else. Why? I think they're pretty, but I don't really understand why they're such a big deal.

You could say boys are always trying to feel and touch them because girls have them and they don't. But we aren't always trying to touch and feel what they've got that we haven't. I did let Peter touch mine once when we were kissing. It wasn't even like he asked and I said yes *or* no. Just suddenly he was touching them, but in a nice friendly way, like he was petting a cat. Mama says sex can make some men wild and mean, but Peter was always so nice when we kissed. I felt sometimes like I could've gone on kissing him for days, it was so nice.

I dried myself off and looked at myself in the long mirror on the back of the door. I think I'm okay. I wouldn't mind all that much if my breasts stayed right the way they are, only I grew another six inches.

When it came time for supper, I shook Mama, but she just mumbled, said she wanted to sleep through and I should meet Nicholas down in the restaurant like we'd planned. I was in my nice dress and sandals. I looked good and even squirted on some of Mama's perfume before I left, the one called Scoundrel. I figured I might as well do it up right, since Nicholas probably isn't used to dining with women my age.

We ate right in the restaurant. It was fancy, with low lights and music in the background and menus so big you couldn't see over them. Mama gave me fifteen dollars so I knew I could have almost anything. I picked fish because I had that once in a restaurant and it was good.

"I guess this is pretty tough on your mother," Nicholas said.

"Yeah, I guess," I said. When I'd gone over to the table, he'd been looking at a photo, but he'd put it in his pocket. "Was that your girl friend?" I said, hoping that wasn't too nosy. Mama says I have a tendency to be nosy, but how can you find out interesting things about people if you don't ask?

"She used to be," Nicholas said. He took the photo out again and showed it to me.

She was a fair-skinned woman with reddish hair, wearing overalls and a plaid shirt. Not what Mama would call someone with style. She looked friendly, though. "Isn't she anymore?" I asked.

"Well, we haven't seen each other in a year. A lot can happen in a year. She was pre-med too, and she went straight on, so now she's ahead of me."

"Do you mind?" Mama says men sometimes mind if women get ahead, no matter if it's by fair means or foul.

23

He shook his head.

"Did you write her while you were away?" I thought of that because I promised to write to Jean-Claude and I haven't yet. I will, maybe tonight even. I'll get a postcard in that store in the lobby.

"I'm not too good at letter writing," he admitted.

"So you think maybe she's got another boyfriend?"

"Could be."

I told him how I was scared of that, too, with Peter. "He's good-looking, and Mama says good-looking men don't let grass grow under their feet." Then I felt bad because Nicholas isn't that good-looking. He's short, a couple of inches shorter than Mama, and he has a friendly face, but that's about all.

"You've got to trust people, Bizou," he said.

"Yeah?" The thing is, Peter never told me he *wouldn't* have any girl friends once he got back, and I never told him *I* wouldn't have any boyfriends. How can you? I didn't know then that I'd be coming to this country six months later. I thought maybe we wouldn't see each other for ten years, even. What I imagined was by then I might be an international photographer like my father, and Peter might be an astronomer, like he said he wanted to be.

Mama thinks it's okay for me to be a photographer, but she doesn't want me to be the kind my father was because that's how he got killed. But if there's a war and you're working for a paper and they send you to shoot pictures, you have to go. Not everyone who goes gets killed. He was just unlucky. Well, I don't argue with her, but I'm going wherever they send me. Maybe by then people won't be having wars anymore. Mama says don't count on it. I don't like to hurt her feelings, but I'd never wanted to be like her friend

Pierre, who took fashion photos. Just women standing around looking fancy. That's not where the action is, in my opinion.

Nicholas and I had a good dinner. The food was good, and I think I was a good dinner companion. I tried not to monopolize the conversation. Mama says with men you have to draw them out and put them at their ease, but sometimes I forget and just start talking a blue streak. "Did you have a good time?" I asked him when we were done.

He said he had. Then we said how we'd meet in the morning for breakfast, and I went up to our hotel room. Mama was still sleeping. I was real quiet so as not to disturb her. It took me a while to get to sleep. What I mostly wished was that when she woke up she'd be in a good mood, like usual.

Chapter 4

But at breakfast Mama said she didn't feel like any more sight-seeing. "You go on and take Bizou," she said to Nicholas. "If you want."

"You sure?" he said. "I know some good places we could go. It might get your mind off things."

Mama said no, she'd just be a drag on us, and she still felt tired. She thought maybe it was the time change. I didn't feel the time change at all. I'd look at my watch and think what time it was in Paris, but my body was all readjusted to the new time. Mama said that was because children adjust faster. I forgave her for referring to me as a child.

We had a good day, Nicholas and me. He took me more places, like up to Columbia University where he went to college and met that girl, Tara, the one he's not sure likes him anymore. He showed me the building he lived in, boys and girls together, even sharing the same bathroom. I don't know if I'd like that!

We walked through Riverside Park and saw some big boats going back and forth. Nicholas said the water was dirty because of pollution, but you couldn't tell to look at it. It smelled a little fishy, but water always does when there's fish in it. I like that smell.

Mama had said she'd meet us at the Statue of Liberty at four so that's where we ended up. We climbed up to the top and looked out, but mainly what you saw was lots of water. I got a postcard to send Jean-Claude. He's going to college in America, he says, if his mother says it's okay. It was past four when we got down. We didn't see Mama so we sat on a bench and waited. Nicholas was getting quiet, with that expression grown-ups get when they want to think and not have you ask questions, so I didn't. I just sat and looked around at some kids playing a little way off.

Four-thirty came and still Mama hadn't showed. She can do that. She doesn't like wearing a watch, except when she's working, so sometimes she forgets all about what time it is. "Maybe she went back to sleep," I said.

"Yeah, maybe I should call the hotel," Nicholas said.

We did that, but there was no answer in the room. So we waited around some more till five o'clock. Then Nicholas called the hotel again and there still wasn't any answer. He asked the man at the front desk if there was a message for anyone in Room 201 or 506—those were our two rooms. The man said there was. Nicholas said he should read them to him on the phone. The man said he couldn't. I figured that out from how mad Nicholas got. He said, "Look, we're waiting for someone and it's extremely important that we get the message— I don't *care* what the rules are!"

When he hung up, he looked mad. "Damn, we'll just have to go back," he said.

"Why can't they read the message on the phone?" I asked.

"Half the rules in the world don't make a bit of sense," he said.

I felt tired by then, though I was glad we'd seen all those things. When we got back to the hotel, the man at the desk took Nicholas aside and said something to him that I couldn't hear. He gave him a letter. Then he came over to me and said there was one for me too. I don't know why I started feeling scared. Maybe because he looked so serious and took Nicholas aside that way. I was scared maybe Mama had been in an accident. Here's what my letter said:

Dear Bizou,
    Honey, I just feel like I've got to get off by myself for a while. You stay with Nicholas and be good, and I'll get in touch with you sometime soon.

                                            Tranquility

Sometime soon! What did *that* mean? And where had she gone? I looked at Nicholas. "What'd she say?" I said, reaching for his letter.

He wouldn't let me read it. "Just . . . I think she felt she needed to get away by herself."

"Why can't I read it?" I felt really upset. "You can read mine."

"You just can't," he snapped. "Okay?"

I started to cry. That's something I never do. Even when Mama hit me once or twice or when my teacher at school, when I was six, stepped on my thumb by mistake, I never cried. But I hated the way Nicholas was acting so snappy, like it was my fault Mama went off like that.

"Listen, I'm sorry," Nicholas said, putting his arm around me.

"She says I should stay with you."

"How can you? I have to . . . School starts in a couple of weeks. I have to see people, get a place to stay."

"So what am I going to do?" I thought at least she must have asked Nicholas before she took off.

He was silent a long time. "Look, I'll tell you what I think is the best thing. Your mother left some money. I'll leave it here with the hotel manager and you stay in the room till she comes back. She won't be gone long."

"How do you know?"

He hesitated. "I don't."

One thing was sure: I wasn't going to cry again, not in front of him anyway. "Okay," I said. "I'll stay here."

"Will you stop looking at me in that accusing way?" Nicholas snapped. "What am I supposed to do? Don't I have a life? I'm supposed to drop everything and cart some kid I never met till three days ago around the country because her mother's too spaced out to bother?"

"I don't *want* you looking after me," I yelled at him. "I can look after myself!" I grabbed my key and went up to Mama's and my hotel room.

Boy, did I feel bad. There's a feeling I get sometimes when I'm just waking up from a bad dream, but the dream still seems true. That's how I felt. Somebody'd come in and fixed up the room so that it was all neat. Mama took all her stuff, though, just left mine. I felt so mad at her that if she'd walked in the door that minute I'd have punched her right in the stomach! Mad at Nicholas too. Mad at the world. What was I supposed to do? It was dinnertime, but I wasn't even hungry. I just lay down on the bed and closed my eyes. Jean-Claude's mother does meditation when she's feeling bad. She says she closes her eyes and tries to imagine a nice place to be, a nice beach or just a scene. She doesn't imagine a story to go with it, just a scene, like you were seeing a movie with no people.

I tried that, but it didn't work. I kept knowing it was me, lying on the bed, pretending I was someplace else. Like when you're in a movie and you just can't get into it for some reason. I didn't even feel like crying. I tried touching myself between my legs because sometimes that can get me sleepy or feeling good, but that didn't work either. Nothing worked! So I just lay there.

There was a knock at the door. "Who is it?" I said. I thought it might be Mama, and I got all ready to pitch into her, but when I opened the door it was Nicholas. "Okay, let's go," he said.

"What do you mean?"

"Listen, I thought it over. I was going to drive up to see Tara anyway. It's a three-, four-hour drive. She'll put us up, we'll stay a few days, we'll keep checking in at the hotel. The minute your mother turns up, we'll come back."

"I don't want to go," I said. It's funny I said that, because I did want to go.

"What do you want to do?" he said, sounding

30

angry again. "Just sit in this hotel room for a week, staring at the walls?"

"Yeah."

"Come on, get your stuff together. We'll talk about it in the car." He began looking for my suitcase. It was under the bed. I knew he wouldn't find it.

"I don't mind being alone," I said. "I like it."

"Don't you think I'm good company?" he said, and smiled.

He reminded me of Peter the way he did that, like knowing I'd say yes. "Pretty good," I said.

He sat down next to me on the bed. "Hey, Bizou, this is kind of tough for me too, okay? Let's just make the best of it."

I got up and started to pack my stuff. He was right. I didn't want to stay in that room all by myself. He checked after me, just the way Mama does, to make sure I remembered everything—my toothbrush, my slippers. I didn't bring a lot of clothes because Mama said we should travel light and I thought I might get some new American clothes here.

I gave my key in at the desk, and Nicholas talked to the hotel manager some more, but the same way, going off so I couldn't hear. That got me mad again. I didn't say a word until we got into this car we rented. It was a small car, and he made me fasten the seat belt. "Aren't you a good driver?" I said.

"Sure, but not everyone else is."

One thing I knew: I wasn't making any conversation or drawing him out or anything. Just because he thinks he's doing me a big favor, taking me along to see his stupid ugly girl friend. But for some reason, when we were on the road I said, "Maybe she jumped off the top of the Empire State Building."

31

Nicholas looked at me. "What do you mean by that?"

"People do."

"Yeah, but what makes you think your mother would?"

"I don't know."

"So why'd you say it?"

I shrugged.

"Has she been feeling depressed a lot lately?" he said.

"Sort of, not all the time." I was sorry I said that. Mama wouldn't do that, I know. She's scared of heights. "Mama wouldn't do that," I said.

"Why not?"

"She's not crazy," I said, looking angrily out the window.

"Wanting to die isn't crazy."

"It is so."

"I've had times I wanted to die. I'm not crazy."

"Maybe you are."

"You think I am?"

I didn't. I knew what I was doing was taking it out on him. This teacher at school said once: become the other person when you're feeling mad, and suddenly you'll see it from their point of view. So I sat there trying to become Nicholas, not even liking kids maybe, wondering why he bothered talking to us on the plane, worrying about his girl friend.

"She probably still likes you," I said finally, just to try to say something nice.

"What?"

"Your girl."

"Oh." He didn't say anything more.

Chapter 5

We stopped off for supper somewhere along the road, not a fancy place, just a diner. That was what it was called: The Diner. I got what Peter says is his favorite meal: a hamburger with French fries and a chocolate malted. It tasted weird, much too sweet.

I didn't bother doing any of that stuff I did the night before, making conversation or anything. In fact, neither of us spoke that much. I asked Nicholas if he had a quarter for me to work the jukebox. He said okay, but only one. I didn't know the songs, so I picked my favorite number: 16. It was a song called "Don't You Want Me" by a group called The Human League. I never heard of them.

We got to Tara's house at 10:07. It's in Vermont. I have a digital watch that my French grandmother gave me when I turned twelve. She's rich, Mama says, but mostly she saves her money and just wears the same dresses over and over. It's funny, Mama says she thinks Nana (that's what I call her, but her real name is Genevieve) has style, but it's in a different way. She says she's "timeless," meaning the way she looks would look good now or maybe a hundred years ago. She has white hair in a chignon, and she stands up straight all the time. She says she hates the way old people stoop. Nana claims that's why they look small, not because they really *are* small. She carries a cane.

I wish Nana wasn't so old and hadn't had a heart attack last year. Otherwise, if Mama never shows, I could go back and stay with her. Maybe I still can. I wouldn't much like living in the country, the way she does, though. Well, I haven't given up on Mama yet. It's just a thought.

"Hi, did you eat?" Tara asked us. She and Nicholas hugged each other a long time when we got out of the car. Maybe she said that just to say something, because most people eat by 10:07. "I have pie," she said. "Want some?"

"Sure," Nicholas said. He looked happy all of a sudden. He still likes her, all right. He smiled at me and winked as we walked into the house.

Tara is quite a good cook, though I still can't get used to American food. I never had a pie like that before, with so much in it, peaches mostly. Also, even though she's not elegant, she's prettier than she looked in the photo. She drags one foot a little when she moves. "I got the guest bedroom ready for you, Eliane," she said to me.

Nicholas was eating a second piece of pie. "This is better than anything in France," he said. "Four stars at least."

Tara beamed at him. "You look skinny. Did you lose a lot of weight?"

"Five pounds, maybe."

I knew the second I was in bed they'd start kissing and hugging. Even though I liked Nicholas and Tara seemed nice, it made me feel lonely and bad again.

The room she called a guest room was funny. I never saw a room like that. The ceiling came down on a slant, and there was wallpaper with bunches of flowers all over the wall, even on the ceiling. There was a big, fluffy blanket like Nana has in her house. "Will you be comfortable?" Tara asked me when I was in bed.

"Yes," I said.

I wanted so bad to fall right asleep. I didn't want to lie there thinking of them being so happy and cuddling up in bed together. Mama and Pierre used to do that after I went to bed, and sometimes I'd hear them. I didn't hear words, but I heard how they sounded happy.

I did fall right asleep, but in the middle of the night I woke up and went to the bathroom down the hall. I passed their room, but the door was closed and everything was quiet. It was quiet outside too, no cars or sounds. I hope Mama's okay wherever she is.

In the morning I woke up early. This time when I passed the room where Tara and Nicholas were, it was open. They were both still in bed, sleeping. That means they're lovers. But they were sleeping just like regular people, turned in opposite directions. Nicholas opened his eyes and saw me. "Good morning," he whispered.

"Good morning," I whispered back.

"I'll be down in a minute."

When he came down, he said, "Sleep okay?"

I nodded. "Did you?"

He just smiled. It got me mad. It's awful when people go around acting that happy when you're not.

"Beez, I was thinking," he began. "Do you have any idea where your mother was planning to go from New York? Did she have plans to see her parents?"

I shrugged.

"Where do they live?"

"I don't know."

"Don't you even know what state they live in?"

It bothered me that he was acting like I was stupid for not knowing. So I told him how Mama never even mentioned them, except to say her father was a doctor, and I told him my theories about why. Nicholas listened carefully. "But wasn't the point of coming back here to see them again?"

"Maybe."

He was silent a long time.

"Why don't we call the hotel?" I suggested. "Maybe she came back."

He started to say something, but stopped. "Okay, let's give that a try."

The hotel man said nothing was different, no message. Just as Nicholas hung up, Tara came downstairs. She was in jeans and a checked shirt.

She fixed breakfast for us, some kind of cereal that tasted funny, and milk. I didn't feel that hungry.

"Maybe Ellie has some friends she could look up," Tara said cheerfully. They both looked at me.

"What do you mean?" I asked.

"Well, you said you went to that American school," Nicholas said. "Do you remember the names of any of the kids who were in your class?"

Of course I did! But I didn't want to tell him. Peter's father works for the State Department, and I was afraid that might get Mama into some kind of trouble. "I'm not sure," I said, not looking at him.

"Maybe she should go back to France," Tara said.

"Her mother said she sublet their apartment," Nicholas said.

"Still," Tara said, "at least she knows people there. She's not a total stranger like she is here."

I hated the way that sounded: a total stranger.

"She knows us," Nicholas said.

"Nick, school starts in three weeks."

"I know it does."

"You've missed a whole year. When are you going to get going?" Tara sounded impatient.

"Relax, okay? I've been in this fucking country four days!"

Tara really looked mad. "Are you just looking for excuses to put everything off?"

"Yeah," Nicholas said. "That's just what I'm doing. I saw this kid and her mother, and I figured: great, this'll kill a few weeks, and maybe if I'm lucky I can find some other excuse."

For a second Tara was silent. "I just think you've been away a long time," she said finally.

"I know," Nicholas said. "I know I have."

I felt bad. I know grown-ups argue with each other, but they'd seemed so happy the night before, and I felt like I'd wrecked it somehow.

"Look, we'll figure something out," Nicholas said. "Meanwhile let's take a walk, okay?"

"I have some letters to write," Tara said, putting the milk away. You could tell she was still mad at him.

"Fine, we'll clear out and leave you a nice quiet house. Want to take a walk, Ellie?"

I nodded.

We walked in a big field with lots of grass and trees. It was wilder than where Nana has her house, and the trees were bigger, but it reminded me a little bit of being there. "I'm sorry you had a fight," I said.

"Me too." He threw a stone far off into the woods. "God, she pisses me off sometimes! So I start a year late! Who *cares*? Will the world collapse if one more little Jewish doctor doesn't roll off the assembly line and start gouging patients for as much money as he can get?"

"Are you Jewish?" I asked.

He nodded.

"My father was," I told him. "He had to hide during the war, in the country."

"Yeah," Nicholas said. "I know."

"How do you know?"

"Your mother told me about him. It sounded like she loved him a lot."

"She did." I looked at him. "Do you love Tara a lot?"

"I used to. I don't know. In ways, but . . . She just wants everyone to be—I don't know, so damned organized and precise, just like *her*. I'm not like that! I'm not asking her to be like *me*. Why should *I* be like her?"

We walked along without saying anything.

"Last night you seemed happy," I said.

He smiled with a funny expression. "Yeah, well . . ."

When we got back around lunchtime Tara didn't seem mad anymore. She kissed Nicholas hello and asked if we'd had a good walk. "Maybe I'll call the hotel again," I said.

Nicholas grabbed my hand. "No. Once a day is enough."

"Why?" I said.

"Because—"

"It can't hurt to call," Tara said.

"I said once a day is enough," Nicholas said in a louder voice.

"We heard you," Tara said. "Will you stop yelling?"

"I wasn't yelling. Ellie, come on, please. Start thinking. You've got to remember the names of some kids you went to school with. Some of them might be back here for vacation."

"There was a boy—" I said.

"Who was he?" Nicholas interrupted. He grabbed my arm and held it tight. "Do you know where he lives?"

"His name was Peter Haynes," I told him. I looked from him to Tara and back again. "He lives on Connecticut Avenue in Washington, D.C."

Chapter 6

Nicholas got hold of Peter's father later that day. I was hoping he wouldn't, that they'd be off somewhere on vacation, in Maine where Peter said they sometimes go in the summer. In a way I almost wished I'd just stayed in the hotel, waiting for Mama. If I'd waited, it would have seemed like I thought she'd be back soon. If I had all the money in the world right now, I'd give it to know where Mama is and what she is doing right this second. Doesn't she know I'm worried sick about her?

"He says we should drive down as soon as we can," Nicholas said.

"What's he going to do?" I asked.

"He might have some contacts that will help. Peter's your friend, isn't he?"

"Yeah, but . . ."

"We'll bunk down with them a few days. If it's a dead end, we'll try something else."

"I think it's going to be a dead end," Tara said.

"Do you have any other suggestions?" Nicholas snapped.

"I'm just a woman," she said sarcastically.

"Give me a break, will you?" Nicholas said.

That night we had supper in Tara's kitchen. She didn't talk much. She put music on so we could listen to that. I still didn't feel that hungry, but I ate a little bit so she wouldn't think I thought she was a bad cook. Afterward we sat in the living room and helped her do a big jigsaw puzzle of a mountain. It had millions of pieces—I never saw one like that. Tara had the part she'd already done at one end of the table and the pieces she couldn't figure out scattered around. Whenever she thought she could see where a piece went, she'd pick it up and fit it in. "Peter Haynes," she said. "I had a boyfriend named Peter once. In high school. Too good-looking. That was his trouble."

Maybe Peter's a bad-luck name. Maybe all boys named that are stuck up and handsome.

"What's wrong with good-looking?" Nicholas said. He was sitting backwards on a chair, leaning forward.

"He had all these slimy cheerleader types fawning all over him all the time," Tara said, fitting in a piece of sky. "It was sick."

"Sounds like heaven," Nicholas said. "God, I really missed out. No slimy cheerleaders, nothing."

"What do you mean—nothing?" I asked him. "Didn't you have any girl friends?"

"Not a one—no one would have me. I was a disaster area. I mean, I know it's hard to realize that now, but I wasn't always this witty, vivacious kind of

41

person. I was a little ugly shrimp of a guy who sat in the corner picking his nose all day."

I burst out laughing, I couldn't help it. There's a boy in my class like that.

"You're just playing on our sympathy," Tara said. "I bet you had *someone*."

"I didn't. Listen, you want to know how hard up I was? I asked Fiona Shapiro to the opera, orchestra seats, fourth row—my parents had a subscription—and she said she'd rather stay home and finish *Jane Eyre*. And Fiona Shapiro weighed a hundred and fifty pounds and was going bald, I swear, at sixteen."

"She sounds great," Tara said. "I think you missed your big chance."

"*I* read *Jane Eyre*," I said. "It was good."

"Orchestra seats!" Nicholas said.

"So what did you do?" Tara asked.

"About what?"

"Did you go alone?"

"No! I cried into my pillow or jerked off or whatever . . . I don't know. I don't think I even knew *how* to jerk off. I was impossibly backward." He grabbed a piece of the puzzle and tried to fit it in; it didn't go. "Fiona Shapiro's probably a high fashion model making two hundred thousand a year now," he said moodily.

"I told you," Tara said. "You missed your chance."

"Maybe she's still finishing *Jane Eyre*," I said.

Nicholas hugged me. "Yeah, that's right. I like that . . . I bet she was just a slow reader."

In bed that night I thought about Peter. If it hadn't been for Mama going off this way, I would've liked to see Peter again. He taught me how to French kiss. I don't know why they call it "French." Mama says that what the French don't know about love and romance isn't worth knowing, so maybe they invented it. It's when you put your tongue in someone's mouth when you kiss them. When Peter explained it, I thought, Gross! And in the beginning I think I didn't do it right. I'd stick my tongue in too far.

I kissed a lot with Jean-Claude too, but he was always horsing around, like we were still babies. I know how he feels. Sometimes, right in the middle of doing it, you suddenly think, How strange, it's me. It's like part of you can't believe you're really doing it.

One thing I'm going to do is be real cool if Peter does have some other girl or girls. I'll pretend I have lots of other boyfriends. Mama didn't like his family. She thought they were snobbish. Mama said rich black people sometimes are worse snobs than white people or anyway just as bad, and it got her mad. Really, I think what got her mad was Peter's mother once saying how she thought our living in Paris was a cop-out, that she thought black people should stay in their own country and try to make things better, not "escape" where it'd be easier. "What does *she* know about escape?" Mama said.

Tara said she wished she could go with us, but she had a lot to do to get ready for school. She said we should call and let her know what happened. She and Nicholas kissed good-bye, a long kiss; maybe they like each other again.

When we were on the road, Nicholas said, "So what do you think? Should I marry her?"

"Yeah!" I said, excited. Maybe I could come to the wedding if they did it now in the next week or so.

"But I want kids and she doesn't, she's neat and I'm a slob, she's an over-achiever and I like to goof off. We'd be screaming at each other all day."

"Maybe you'd better not marry her then," I said. If Nicholas was younger, *I'd* marry him. I think he's cute. He reminds me of Jean-Claude a little. "Did you really not have a girl friend in high school?" I asked.

"Would I make something like that up?" Nicholas smiled at me. "How about you?"

I smiled back. "I have a few."

"Just a few!"

"Two mostly."

"Both the same? Neither one is out in front?"

"What does out in front mean?"

"That's from horse racing," Nicholas explained. "The one out in front is the one who's likely to win."

"So you mean who do I like best?"

"Yeah."

"It's complicated." I looked at him. "Sometimes I'm fickle," I admitted. "I mean, like, I can like Jean-Claude because he's fun to be with, but Peter's better at kissing."

"I know," Nicholas said, sighing.

"How do you know?" I asked. "You never met them!"

"I mean, I know what that's like, liking two people or wanting everything in one person. . . . But you never get it," he said suddenly.

"Mama says you do if you wait and you're choosy."

"Well, she was lucky then."

"I'm going to be lucky too. . . . Isn't Tara a good kisser, or what?"

44

Nicholas laughed. "She's good. . . . How old are you again?"

"Thirteen."

"God, when I was thirteen I was three feet high and trying to glue model airplanes together. I thought kisses were something you ducked when your mother came at you."

"Those kind are different."

"Yeah, I figured that out. But it took me another ten years."

Chapter 7

After we'd been on the road about two hours, I started feeling funny. Nicholas said I could lie down in the back seat, so I crawled over and did. I started remembering a trip I took with Mama once where she drove and I lay in the back seat. I thought maybe if I closed my eyes and concentrated, when I opened them, she'd be there again, but nothing happened except I fell asleep.

When I woke up, Nicholas was still driving. It had started to rain. "We'll stop pretty soon," he said. He was driving slower because we were coming to a bridge. "Hey, look at that girl," he said.

I sat up. "Where?"

He pointed to one side of the car. This girl was standing in the rain in a yellow raincoat with a hood. She was holding a sign saying, "Going South?" She

looked really wet and unhappy. "What do you say?"
Nicholas said.

"What about?"

"Should we pick her up?"

Mama says people who pick up hitchhikers can get
killed, that it's a bad thing to do. But that girl didn't
look harmful. "Okay," I said.

We pulled over and Nicholas opened the window.
"We're going to Washington," he said. "Can we drop
you somewhere?"

For a minute it was like the girl hadn't heard him.
She just stood there with water dripping off her hood.
Then she looked nervously at Nicholas and back at
me. "*Where* are you going?" she said with a stutter.

Nicholas said again, "Washington. Is that along
your route?"

The girl opened the door. "I'm so wet!" she said.
"Nobody would stop, except this truck driver I didn't
like the looks of at *all*. If you and your little girl hadn't
come along, I don't know what I'd have done."

"I'm not his little girl," I said.

"That's Eliane," Nicholas said. "And I'm Nicholas. Her mother's a friend of mine."

The girl turned around and shook my hand. "Could
I take my coat off?" she asked. "I'm just wet
through. . . . I'm Rae."

"What's that short for?" Nicholas asked.

"Raymond . . . I'm in drag." She laughed. "No,
it's just Rae. Why does everything have to be *short* for
something?"

"Where are you headed?" Nicholas said. "Or
rather why?"

"My college starts in a few weeks," she said. "And
I took last year off. So I'm kind of looking around for
a place to stay. Sort of nervous, you know. I'm glad I

47

took the year off, but, like, I'm not sure I'll get into the thing of studying again."

"That's what *he* did," I said.

"Well, I finished college," Nicholas explained, "but I took a year off before med school."

Rae looked at him with interest. "Did you work or what?"

"I was in France."

"Really? How great! I'm going to do that my junior year. I'm a French major. Do you know French?"

The next part was funny. They started speaking French. But, boy, did she have a terrible American accent! I never heard anything so bad. And everything she said came out wrong. I hope I don't sound like that in English. "It gives me pleasure that you are not a murderer," she said in French.

Nicholas said back in French, "We have no desire to molest attractive women."

"Without the child in the back seat my fear would have been too great," she said in French.

Child! I tried not to burst out laughing, by putting my hand over my mouth.

"Uh, Eliane is French," Nicholas said in English.

"Oh, wow." Rae turned to me again. She switched back to English. "My accent's terrible, right? But I think my grammar is getting a lot better. I've been reading all these French novels. The trouble is, the high school I went to, the French teacher was from Brooklyn. So I never learned how to speak the right way."

"My French teacher was from Brooklyn too," Nicholas said. "Where'd you go?"

"Oh, it's this weird little private school in New

York—Marlow. Nobody ever heard of it. It's kind of—"

Nicholas laughed. "I went there."

"You *did*?"

"Yeah, Class of '77."

"God, that's incredible!" Rae said. To me she said, "I never even met anyone who *heard* of it." She turned back to Nicholas. "And you really got through college? That's encouraging."

"It was tough. . . . So did you go all the way through? You must have been in seventh grade when I was a senior."

"Your class did *The Birthday Party* for the senior play," Rae said.

"I was Goldberg."

"You were great!" To me she said, "He was really terrific. He played this villain, and he really made you hate him. . . . Who was the girl who played the woman you were so mean to?"

"Lotta King."

"That's right. God, this is so amazing! It's like once I met someone who lived in the same apartment I used to live in with my parents before they split."

She asked where we were going, and Nicholas said we were going to stay with a friend of mine from school. I was glad he didn't mention about Mama, even though Rae seemed really friendly and nice.

"Is your mother black?" she asked me.

I nodded.

"My sister's going with a black guy, and my mother's kind of freaked out about it. Of course she freaks out about a lot of stuff, but . . . She says it won't be fair to their kids. Was it okay for you?"

"Sure," I said.

"She grew up in France," Nicholas said.

"You said you were just there for a year," Rae said.

"That was me," Nicholas said.

"Oh, I thought you and her mother were traveling around together."

"We just met on the plane coming back," Nicholas said.

"I get it, kind of," Rae said. She shut her eyes. "Boy, I'm bushed. Is it okay if I don't talk? I don't want to be rude, but I'm so tired."

She fell asleep in about two seconds. She snored even, just like Nana. Nicholas looked over at her. "Cute."

When we stopped for dinner, it was late, around eight. All of a sudden I felt starving. Rae said she'd eat with us. After dinner she asked how much farther we'd be going that night.

"I thought we might stop off here," Nicholas said, "and get an early start in the morning."

She was silent a minute. "Could I—um—sleep in your car? Would you mind?"

"You can share our room."

"I don't have much money," Rae explained, "and I want to make it last as long as I can."

There was a whole row of little cabins. Nicholas told the lady at the desk we wanted one, with an extra cot for me. The lady looked at me suspiciously. "This your little girl?" she said.

"Yeah," Nicholas said. "She's mine."

I didn't get why he lied about that.

"How old is she?"

"Thirteen."

"And she"—she pointed at Rae—"is your wife?"

"No," Nicholas said. "She's a friend."

50

"They went to school together," I said.

"Well, she has to have a separate room," the lady said.

"Who?" Nicholas said impatiently. I could tell he was getting mad.

"I'm sorry, mister. We don't allow three in a room."

Rae went over and touched Nicholas on the arm. "Hey, listen, I'll sleep in the car, it's okay."

"Relax," he said. To the lady he said, "What's the problem? Could you let us in on it? Are you afraid of some giant orgy? Spell it out for us, okay, because we're a little naïve."

"If you were married . . ." the lady began.

Nicholas laughed. "Bizou here's only thirteen," he said. "I think that's a little young for marriage."

"Nick, really," Rae said. "I've slept in cars *lots* of times."

Nicholas turned back to the woman at the desk again. "Look, will having her sleep in a car and get a lousy night's sleep mean so much to you? She's been traveling all day, she's exhausted—"

"*I* can sleep in the car," I said.

Nicholas threw up his hands. "No one's sleeping in the car! Got it? Either we all stay here or we move on. So how about it, lady?"

The lady looked uncertain.

"Let's go somewhere else," Rae said.

"Okay," Nicholas said. "Thanks a lot for your hospitality. We really appreciate it."

Just as he turned away, the lady called out, "Here. Take Cabin Four. Checkout time is eleven a.m."

Nicholas just looked at her. He opened his mouth,

started to say something, and then took the key. We started down to Cabin Four.

"I brought you bad luck," Rae said mournfully.

"*She* was bad luck," Nicholas said. "I would've liked to make a grand exit, but I'm too bushed."

"Maybe it was me," I said. I thought of how Mama said in America some people get mad if a black person and a white person are together or have children together.

"It's a waste of time trying to figure it out," Nicholas said. He opened the door to the cabin. "*Voilà!* It's not the Grand Ballroom of the Waldorf, but what can you do?"

"I *would've* slept in the car," Rae said, taking off her coat. "Really."

"If you say that one more time, kid, we'll tie you to the roof of the cabin," Nicholas said, laughing.

I giggled.

"It's just—" Rae began, but there was a knock at the door. I was scared it was the lady, changing her mind again, but it was a man carrying a cot. He unfolded it and put it in a corner of the room. Then he showed us where the sheets and blankets were.

"I can take the cot," Rae said when the man went away. There were two other beds.

The cot didn't look that comfortable, so I said okay. I got into my nightgown, but they just stayed with their clothes on. We tried watching TV, but it was broken. I guess I fell asleep then, because when I woke up again, it was morning and Nicholas was sleeping in the other bed and Rae was sleeping in the cot.

We dropped her off in a city called Baltimore.

"Hey, you guys really saved my life," she said. "Thanks."

"For someone who thought I was great in the senior play, there are no lengths to which I wouldn't go," Nicholas said.

"Have a good life," she said, and waved at us as we drove off.

That's a funny expression: have a good life.

"Did you like her?" I asked Nicholas. I'd moved into the front seat again.

"On a scale of one to five . . . three."

"Would you want her for a girl friend if you didn't have Tara?"

"Maybe . . . I don't know. She was kind of young, a little—" He made a gesture.

"A little what?"

"Spacy. I guess she wasn't my type so much."

Peter used to say that about me—that I wasn't his type. He said his type was curvy blond girls who were more melty and sweet. He said I was sweet and sour, like Chinese spareribs.

Chapter 8

Before we got to Peter's house, I said to Nicholas, "I'm scared Peter's father could get Mama into trouble."

"How?"

"He works for the American government. They're bad people."

"Not all of them. Look, we'll play it by ear."

"Tranquility thought Peter's parents were snobbish. She didn't like them. I think she'd be mad if she knew we were doing this."

"Well, she shouldn't have gone off then," Nicholas said in an irritated voice.

"I should've stayed back at the hotel," I said. "She'd probably be back by now if I had."

"That doesn't make any sense," Nicholas said.

"Take me back," I told him. "I want to go back now."

"No way," Nicholas said. "I didn't drive all the way down here for nothing. We decided to do this, and we're going to. Got it?"

"You're bossy," I told him, moving over by the window.

"So're you!"

"So what're you going to do?" I said, glaring at him. "Just leave me there?"

"No, I'll hang around till arrangements are made for you."

"What arrangements?" I got really scared. "Are you going to put me in an orphanage?"

"Ellie, cool it. You're not an orphan. Why should they put you in an orphanage?"

"I want to go back to France."

"Look, you want a lot of things. But I can't just ship you back when you don't have a place to stay."

If only Mama hadn't sublet our apartment, I could just go back and stay there till she came. I could have meals with Jean-Claude and read and take walks. Nicholas reached over and squeezed my hand. "Don't worry, promise?"

I just looked at him. How can you promise not to worry? That's dumb.

Peter's family lived in an apartment house. You had to drive up to this fancy entrance, and in the lobby there was a man in a uniform who asked where you were going. I wished so much I hadn't told Nicholas I remembered anyone in my class. Maybe I'm going to get Mama and me into terrible trouble.

A maid in a uniform answered the doorbell, which rang with pretty chimes, like birds. She told us to sit in the living room till Mrs. Haynes came out. That's Peter's mother.

It was a big living room, like the one they had in Paris. A light yellow rug ran all across it, and pictures were everywhere on the walls. Nicholas sat down at one end of the couch. He looked uncomfortable. Maybe he was afraid he wasn't dressed fancily enough. He just had on jeans and a short-sleeved checked shirt. I knew I looked good. I was wearing my white dress with the black polka dots. I washed it the night we were at Tara's, so it's still fresh-looking, and I've been bathing almost every night, like Mama says I should. Even though I'm mad at her for running off, I want her to be proud of me.

"Why, hello, Eliane," Peter's mother said, coming into the room. She came over and hugged me. "It's so lovely to see you again." Nicholas stood up and shook her hand. She is in between pretty and not. She's a little heavy—"stately," Mama used to call her—and she has this kind of smile where you don't know how sincere it is. Mama says she probably smiles in her sleep. "Peter wanted so much to be here when you arrived," she said, "but he has a job this summer. He's helping his father out in the office."

She sat down in a chair near me. "So how've you been enjoying our country? This weather is just . . . I hate July more than anything."

"I like it," I said.

"I'm so glad you called us," Mrs. Haynes said. "My husband is just the person to turn to in a crisis like this. He knows everyone in Washington."

That's just what I was afraid of. Nicholas said, "I don't think there's any reason to get alarmed at this point."

"Of course not," Mrs. Haynes said. "Anyway, you don't have to worry about that with Charles. He *never* gets alarmed. But he'll find your mother if anyone can."

"She's planning on coming back," I said quickly. "She just wanted to go off to be by herself for a while."

"I know just how she feels!" Mrs. Haynes said. "Don't we all?"

"She just doesn't like it here," I went on. "Some bad things happened."

I looked at Nicholas. He said, "Just some incidents. It was my fault, really. I was showing Ellie and her mother some sights, and there were a few men who . . . called out some ugly things."

Mrs. Haynes pressed her lips together. "Well, that does happen," she said. "But it's only one side of things."

"I know," Nicholas said.

"There are good things too," she rushed on. "You can't judge by a single incident. Goodness, look at the French! I won't even *tell* you all the run-ins I had over there. But you learn to accept different customs, different ways of doing things. You adapt."

"Yeah," Nicholas said.

Then Peter's mother showed us where we could stay. They sure had a lot of rooms! I was in a room with a big bed and a mirror right across from it, like the kind Mama uses to put on her makeup. Nicholas got some other room just as big and fancy. Peter said it wasn't so much that his parents were rich, but it was part of his father's job to entertain a lot. Mama went to one of their parties and said most of the people were a lot of stuffed shirts and she almost fell asleep standing up.

When Peter came home, I almost didn't recognize

him. I guess even if you remember someone in your mind, it's different when you see them. I think he must have grown some since we last met because he was way taller than me. I was sorry because he always used to call me "Shrimp," just to be teasing, but it still bothered me. I'm going to catch up someday.

"Hi," he said. His smile was friendly, like he was glad to see me.

Then we just stood there, not knowing what to say. Peter's father suggested Peter show me his room. I had the feeling that was so he could talk to Nicholas without us around. Peter's father is tall, too, and heavy. He reminds me of a ship. He has a big booming kind of loudspeaker voice.

"I was really surprised when Mom said you were coming," Peter said. "Are you in some kind of trouble or what?"

"No!" I said.

"Mom said your mother got in some kind of trouble."

"She didn't." I felt bad at the idea of Peter's mother talking about Tranquility that way. Like Tranquility says, she's managed all on her own. She doesn't have any husband with a big fancy job to take care of her. She's made it the hard way. "She just went off for a while . . . and pretty soon she'll come back."

"Oh." He looked uncomfortable.

"So do you have a new girl friend yet?" I said, just to change the subject. I know I said I wouldn't ask that, but what's the point of not asking something you want to know?

He looked embarrassed. "Kind of . . . Not so much."

I marched up to him. "Which one? Kind of or not so much?"

"There's this girl who kind of likes me—Danny. She's okay, nothing so special. How about you?"

I just shrugged.

"I bet you started going around with J.C. again right after I left, huh?"

"We're just 'kind of' friends mostly," I said sarcastically.

"That's what it's like with me and Danny," Peter said. "Mostly friends."

"You don't kiss her or anything?"

"Sometimes, but it's not—"

"So she's your girl friend!" I said, really mad. I walked off to the window and looked out.

"I told you she wasn't!"

"So what did you kiss her for?"

"She likes me to."

Boy, I felt so mad I wished I wasn't even there, seeing him. "You're just like Mama said," I said. "You'd kiss a turtle, I bet!"

Peter came over and put his arms around me. "Well, maybe, if its shell wasn't so hard."

"*I'm* not a turtle," I said. I felt confused because I liked it when he hugged me. He started kissing my forehead.

"Ellie, don't be mad," he said. "Come on. Look up at me."

"What if your mother comes in?"

He went over and locked the door. Then we sat down on the floor and kissed a little. But it was funny. Even though I liked it, part of me was still worried about Mama and what was going to happen. I couldn't concentrate on it. Then all of a sudden there was a knock on the door. Peter jumped up, and so did I. He went to unlock it.

"Danny's on the phone," Peter's mother called out cheerfully. To me she said, "My husband wants to talk to you a little bit, Eliane. Why don't you come in and join us?"

I went back into the living room, but as I went I tried to listen to what Peter was saying on the phone. I bet anything he's lying. I bet he does like Danny and she's his real official girl friend. I wish so much I hadn't kissed him, right off like that. Mama says if men think you're easy, they don't respect you. I'm not easy, I'm hard! But I still like kissing Peter a lot. The way he smells and feels is good. It's hard to explain.

Chapter 9

I thought Peter's father was going to speak to me with Nicholas and Peter's mother there, but instead he took me into his study and had me sit in this leather chair while he sat behind his desk. It got me really nervous.

"Nicholas says he met you and your mother on the plane coming over from Paris. Is that correct?"

I nodded. "I met him first because Mama was asleep."

"And you'd never met him before? He wasn't a friend of your mother's at any previous time in her life?"

"Uh-uh."

"How certain are you of that, Eliane?"

I didn't get what he meant. "He was on the plane," I said. "He was going to go to medical school, but he took a year off and his grandparents paid for it."

"How do you know that?"

"He told me."

"But, to the best of your knowledge, you never saw him before that plane trip?"

"Yes!" Boy, he was weird. I told him that already about five times!

"The reason I'm probing into this aspect of it is it seems a little strange to me that your mother would leave you with a man she scarcely knew. Wouldn't she be concerned about what kind of person he was, if, in fact, she had barely met him a few days earlier?"

"Mama decides right off if she likes people or not," I said. "Nicholas is a good person. You don't have to worry about that."

"I believe that's true. But it still strikes me as strange that she would entrust her child with a man who—"

"She doesn't know that many people here," I interrupted him.

"How about her family?"

My heart started beating hard. Even if they torture me, I'm not going to say anything to get Mama into trouble. They can pour honey on me and let ants eat me, but I won't. "She doesn't get along so well with her family."

"But she maintains contact with them?"

I shrugged.

"Doesn't she write them, talk to them on the phone?"

I shook my head slowly.

"You've never seen a letter from anyone in your mother's family? A sister? A brother? No one?"

"I never did," I said. That's the truth.

"And your mother has no friends she's kept in touch with that you know of?"

"Uh-uh."

Mr. Haynes stared off in space, frowning. "What do you think the purpose of this visit was then, Eliane?"

"Just to, like, show me America, what it was like."

"So the plan was to travel around, see different parts of the country?"

I nodded.

"Did your mother say which parts? Mention any particular states she wanted to show you?"

"She said we'd mostly play it by ear."

He was silent a long time. Finally he said, "Why do *you* think your mother disappeared?"

The word "disappeared" didn't sound good to me. "She didn't 'disappear'!" I said, trying not to sound mad. "She just went off . . . to be by herself, to think about things."

"Has she done that before?"

"Not exactly."

"What do you mean, 'not exactly'?"

I kept having the feeling he was trying to trap me some way. I wondered if he was taping our conversation. "No, she never went off before," I mumbled.

"Are you worried about her?"

I didn't say anything.

"It would be perfectly natural to be worried," he said.

"She's coming back," I cried. "I'm *not* worried."

"You're not worried she may have had an accident or tried to . . . Nicholas said you said something about her jumping off a bridge."

I felt really bad, having said that. "That was a joke," I said.

"Did you ever feel maybe your mother was so depressed she really would do something like that?"

"No," I whispered. But it was hard for me to talk, I felt so bad.

Then we just sat there, Mr. Haynes looking at me and me looking at his desk. "Okay," he said finally. "Well, we can talk some more tomorrow. Why don't we just relax and have some dinner now? I don't want to tire you out, dear."

All during dinner I kept thinking back on the conversation I'd had with Peter's father, hoping I didn't say anything wrong. When Mama comes back, I'm going to give her a real talking-to. I can tell you one thing: I'm not going through this again. She better never, ever do this again or I'll never speak to her, *ever*.

Peter has two younger brothers, Mark and Roe. Mark's nine and Roe's seven. I remember them from Paris. They don't look like Peter that much. Roe is kind of chubby and loud, and Mark's smart and skinny. Dinner was really good. Crispy chicken and potatoes that were perfect and strawberries with cake and ice cream for dessert. This lady served it and came around twice in case you wanted seconds. I didn't know if it would be polite to take seconds, but Peter and his brothers did so I did too.

After supper we went into this room to watch TV. I couldn't pay so much attention to the show. I sat there, but I wasn't really concentrating on it.

"I still remember French," Mark said. "Daddy makes us take lessons." He said something in French, but I couldn't understand it.

"Is your mommy dead?" Roe said.

Peter socked him. "Don't be dumb. Bizou's just visiting us."

"You said she jumped off a bridge."

"I didn't! God, you get everything wrong."

"*I* jumped off a bridge once," Roe said to me.

"Which bridge?" Mark said sarcastically.

"We made it in school," Roe said. "It was tall. . . . Are you Peter's girl friend?"

"No," I said.

"But you were before," he said. "I saw you kissing once."

"Go to bed, will you?" Peter said. He threw a pillow at him. "It's late."

"I'm not tired." Roe turned to me. "I kissed Alison on Valentine's Day and she started to cry."

"I don't blame her," Mark said.

Peter's mother looked in. "How are things going?" she asked.

"Mom, take him away, will you? He's bothering us."

"Will you be here in the morning?" Roe said.

I nodded.

"I didn't like France," he said. "It was dirty. I'm glad we're back here." He followed his mother out of the room.

"We should have left him over there," Mark said.

Peter said, "Don't mind what he said, Ellie. He's a jerk."

"I don't," I said.

Peter was sitting right next to me, but I knew he wouldn't do anything with Mark there. "Do *you* have a girl friend?" I asked Mark.

"No, I'm not into girls yet."

65

Peter laughed. "All *he* likes is spaceships."

"I'm going to be the first black man on the moon," Mark said.

After a while Peter's mother came in again and said Mark had to go to sleep. "Maybe you and Eliane should start pretty soon too," she said to Peter.

"Relax, Mom," he said. "We're teenagers. We don't have to go to bed at nine!"

"Eliane is our guest. If her mother were here, she'd want her to get a good rest."

After she left, Peter said in a whisper, "Maybe I'll come in your room later."

"How can you? Don't they stay up late?"

"Not later than ten usually."

"I don't know," I said. Part of me would've liked him to, but I thought how if Peter's mother caught us doing anything, kissing even, she'd hit the roof and blame Tranquility for not having given me a regular home.

"Don't you like me anymore?" he said.

"You know I do," I said crossly. "Just don't *pressure* me, okay?"

"Okay," Peter said meekly. We sat in silence a minute. Then he said, "Tomorrow I'll show you all around. Maybe when your mother comes back, you can live here and go to my school. What do you think?"

I was glad he put it that way, like he thought Mama would be back soon. "I'd like that a lot," I said, and kissed him quick, then jumped up and went in to wash up.

Chapter 10

But when I was in bed, I got a spooky, scared feeling. Maybe it was partly because it was such a big room and the mirror across from the bed reflected things. Every time a car passed, the light would trace over the mirror like someone with a flashlight searching for someone. I ducked down under the covers and tried putting the top sheet over my eyes, but I still felt funny. Then I got really scared. The door of my room opened, slowly, and someone started creeping across to the window. I thought it might be Peter, even though I'd told him not to, but I wasn't sure. Whoever it was went over to where my clothes were, on the chair, and started looking through them.

"Hey!" I whispered.

The person looked up. It was Roe.

"What're you doing in here?"

"I don't know." He looked scared.

"What do you mean you don't know?"

"I was just looking for something."

"What?" Now that I wasn't scared anymore, I felt mad. "What're you looking for? You tell me or I'm going to tell your mama right this second!"

I never would've done that, but I must've scared him because he whispered, "Your bra."

I couldn't help giggling. "What for?"

Roe looked ashamed. "Mark said he'd pay me five dollars if I could steal your bra."

"I don't wear one."

"Really?"

"Yeah. . . . What'd he want my bra for, anyway?"

"I don't know. He collects them or something. You know, like I collect baseball cards?"

"Weird," I said.

"Yeah, he's weird all right," Roe agreed. "I'm sorry if I scared you."

"That's okay."

He started padding out of the room. He was wearing pajamas with red giraffes all over them. Then at the door he turned. "How come you don't wear a bra?" he said, puzzled.

"I don't like them."

"Oh. . . . Well, good night."

"Good night," I called after him.

After Roe left, I felt wide-awake, like I'd never get to sleep at all. When the door opened again, I wasn't even startled. I just sat straight up with the blanket around me. "Who is it?"

"Me," Peter said, closing the door behind him.

"I told you not to come," I said. I felt mad that he hadn't paid any attention, but excited that he was there.

Peter came over and sat on the bed. He was in cotton pajamas, the regular kind. "I just wanted to kiss you good night," he said with a real innocent expression.

"We did before." I looked at him suspiciously.

"Come on. . . . Just once more. Ellie, we might not see each other for a long, long time."

"I thought you said I could go to your school."

"Yeah, but what if your mother doesn't show up? They'll probably send you back to France or something."

"She's *going* to show up." Then I felt Peter's hand starting to reach up under my pajama top. "Hey, Peter, come *on*! I mean it. Be nice."

He took his hand right away. "Okay, let's just kiss one more time, please?"

"Oh, okay." I pretended to be doing it just as a special favor.

We kissed a long time. I was glad I brushed my teeth extra hard. I have to admit it was exciting, doing it in the dark like that with both of us just in our pajamas. But I was good. I didn't go any further than I thought I should. Mama says deciding how far to go is up to each individual and there aren't any rules that'll guarantee your getting what'll make you happy. Maybe if I thought I really would see Peter again soon, it'd be different, but what's the point in getting to like someone a whole lot and then—bingo!— they're gone. And that Danny waiting for him at school, "kind of" friends or whatever.

When Peter went back to his room, I got out of bed. It wasn't that I thought anyone would come in, but I just didn't feel at all sleepy. I sat in a chair near the window and looked out. I started thinking back on

Peter's father questioning me and how tomorrow there'd be more of the same. What got me was how he'd ask things like he thought I was hiding something. I wasn't! But it was like he didn't trust me.

Then I thought of the money Nicholas had that Mama had left with him. I don't know how much it is, but it must have been a lot if it would've paid for the hotel. I thought about it a long time. I'm not a thief, but that money really belongs to me. I decided to take it and get out of this house and hitchhike, like Rae did, back to New York City. I'd check back into the hotel and wait there till Mama comes back. I bet that's what she'd have wanted me to do.

I got dressed quietly and slowly opened the door to my room. I hadn't unpacked much. I carried my suitcase with me and went down the hall to the room Nicholas was sleeping in. I crossed my fingers, praying he'd be asleep.

He was. He was making that heavy breathing sound people do when they sleep. He didn't move at all when I opened the door. I tiptoed as quietly as I could over to the closet and opened the closet door, then closed it tight behind me. Nicholas's jacket was hanging right in front. I felt in all the pockets. I know where he keeps his money because I've seen where he reaches when he pays for tolls. I took out all there was. There were four hundred-dollar bills and some smaller ones. I figured the hundreds must be Mama's, but because Nicholas had been good to me and he might need something, I only took three hundreds and a few smaller bills. I put them in my pocketbook. Then I opened the closet door again very slowly.

Maybe it was the way I opened it or the sound of the

light in the closet clicking off again, but all of a sudden Nicholas sat up and said, "Who's that?"

I stood there, my heart thumping so loud it felt like a drum. "It's me."

"Bizou?"

I nodded.

"What are you doing?"

"I just felt . . . lonely."

"So what were you doing in the closet?"

"Nothing."

Nicholas sat up. "Come on over here," he said, but in a friendly voice. He patted the bed for me to sit down. I did. "What's going on?" he asked.

"I want to go home . . . I don't like it here."

"Home where?"

"Paris."

"So what were you doing in the closet?"

I hesitated. "I thought I could use Mama's money and go back to New York, and if she didn't show up, I'd buy me a ticket home and wait for her there."

"How'd you intend to make it from here to New York?"

"Hitchhike, like Rae."

Nicholas whistled. "Baby, come on, you know better than that. It's dangerous to hitchhike."

"*She* did it."

"It's still not a smart thing to do."

I sat there, looking across the room. "I don't like it here."

"Peter's father giving you a hard time?"

"I don't like him questioning me, like he thinks I'm a liar."

"He doesn't think that." Nicholas looked at me. "It's just—what else is there to do? You say you

71

can't think of anyone your mother knew whom she might've turned to."

I sat there, thinking. What came into my mind was an envelope Mama had that she trimmed out. She cut off the back part and pasted it in her address book. I remembered it because I wondered why she was doing that instead of rewriting it. When I asked her who it was, she said a friend she used to know, "Anita." I kept seeing that name, "Anita," and trying to remember the rest of it. What I remember is that her last name was the same as the name of the street she lived on. It was the name of a tree.

"What're you thinking about?" Nicholas said.

"Sh," I said. "I'm concentrating." I started thinking of every tree I ever saw where I learned the American name. It was the kind of tree you hang decorations on for Christmas. Then I remembered it. Anita Pine. Pine Street. I told Nicholas.

He frowned. "Yeah, but where? Just Pine Street isn't going to help. What was the other part of the address?"

I thought some more, concentrated as hard as I could, but I couldn't remember the rest. Then I started to cry. I felt so tired and discouraged about everything. Nicholas patted my shoulder. "Baby, listen, it doesn't matter. We'll find some other way. We don't have to stay here if you don't want to."

"I remember the number," I said, frowning, not sure if that would help.

"What number?"

At the end there was a number, at the bottom of the envelope. "One nine . . ."

"That must've been the zip code." Nicholas looked pleased. "Good work, Beez. That'll give us the state

72

and maybe we can try and pin it down more closely. You keep thinking about that envelope, and maybe the rest of it'll come to you."

"Can we go now?" I said, excited.

"Now?"

I nodded. "If we wait till morning, Peter's father'll start in questioning us again."

Nicholas thought a minute. "Hon, I need a little more sleep, okay? Especially if we have a lot of driving. Go back to your room. We can set out around five or six, before anyone's awake. We'll leave them a note."

"How'll you make sure to wake up then?"

"Don't worry—I've never used alarm clocks. I can do it."

I hoped that was true. I went back to my room and tried to fall asleep myself. But I didn't sleep much. I'd sleep in little bits and pieces, then start awake, afraid Nicholas had overslept. When he came in at five-thirty, I was wide-awake.

"Let's go," he said.

Chapter 11

We stopped for breakfast at another of those diner places. I was really hungry and had a big breakfast bun and milk. It wasn't as good as a croissant, but I was too starving to care. Nicholas had eggs and toast. Then we went into the phone booth and made about a million calls. Nicholas had figured out Anita Pine must live in Pennsylvania, and he began calling a lot of towns with that zip code. I felt really proud of myself for remembering. I'm good at numbers. Even when I was little, I was. I'd remember them for no reason, numbers of rooms we stayed at or numbers on cars. I don't like numbers especially, though I'm good at math, but they just seem to stick in my brain somewhere.

But Nicholas began looking discouraged after he called lots of places and there wasn't any Anita Pine or even A. Pine. "Maybe she got married," I said.

"Shit." He sat staring off into space. "Who *is* Anita Pine, anyway?"

"I don't *know*!"

"Beez, think. You remembered that number. Try to think back to the conversation, when your mother trimmed out the envelope. What'd she say?"

I wish I was as good at remembering conversations as I am at remembering numbers. "She said she was a friend."

"Go on. What else?"

"I think she said from school . . . something about school. . . . Maybe she said she was a teacher."

"Well, which was it?" Nicholas said impatiently. "Did she go to school with her or was she a teacher?"

"Stop acting mad! I'm thinking!" It was funny, but I kept seeing that scene, Mama's hands trimming the envelope, me sitting there eating a peach. There was a sentence Mama said just as she turned the scissors to go around the bend. Then all of a sudden it came to me. "She said, 'I wonder if she's still at Swarthmore.'" I said it in French because that was how Mama said it.

Nicholas looked so happy I thought he was going to dance. "Did she say *at* Swarthmore or *teaching* at? Think!"

I sighed. My brain was worn out from thinking. "I can't remember."

"Where did you get the idea that she might have been a teacher?"

"I don't know."

"Okay, well, let's try that first." Nicholas tried some more numbers connected with that name I gave him. He said it was a college, and if she was on the faculty or was a student there, she'd be listed. But she wasn't. Then he tried Swarthmore just as a place to live. "Is there anyone under the name of Pine?" he said. "Anita Pine? A. Pine? . . . Spelled any way. P-y-n-e? There's an A. P-y-n-e? . . . Great. Give it to me."

"It wasn't P-i-n-e?" I said.

"It's worth a try," Nicholas said.

He let the phone ring a long time. No one answered. We went back to our table. Nicholas had another cup of coffee, and I had another roll. "This is it," Nicholas said. "I just have a feeling."

"I thought it said P-i-n-e," I said, licking the icing off the bun.

When Nicholas sat down in the phone booth again, he smiled nervously up at me. "Keep your fingers crossed, Beez," he said.

I did, so hard I was afraid they might stick that way, like a pretzel.

Someone must have answered, because Nicholas said, "Is this Anita Pyne? . . . It is? Oh, great. That's wonderful. I'm so glad we got to you. . . . No, I'm a friend of someone I think you know: Tranquility? . . . Yes, she's over here now. Did you know she was coming? . . . Well, her daughter and I are traveling together, and we're not too far from where you live. We wondered if . . . terrific! No, any time. That's swell. We'll see you soon." When he hung up, Nicholas jumped up and hugged me hard. "It's her!"

"I heard you," I said, laughing. But I felt excited too. "What did she say? Did she know we were coming over? Has she heard from Mama?"

"I didn't want to get into everything on the phone.

76

She knew she was coming over here, but she didn't know exactly when, so they must've been in touch fairly recently."

"But if Mama didn't call her, what good will it do?"

"Do you have any other suggestions?" Nicholas said wearily.

"No, but—"

"Anita Pyne is going to be our salvation," Nicholas said. He was in such a good mood I decided not to say anything further. That's how Mama can get when she's in love—all vague and happy and forgetting what the odds are.

When we were in the car, driving again, I asked Nicholas, "What do you think she'll look like?"

"Who?"

"Anita Pyne. Don't you ever do that, imagine ahead of time, then see if you're right?"

"Not usually. Let's see. Anita sounds like—black hair, Spanish-looking. She's going to come swooping out with castanets in her hands, clicking her heels, shouting, '*Olé*.'"

I sighed. "Seriously."

"And Pyne? . . . Well, I see someone tall and thin with shaggy branches and a nice smell, maybe with a star on top of her head."

I could tell he wasn't even *trying* to be serious. "Well, *I* think," I said, "that she'll have brown skin, about like Mama's, and black hair, and she'll be real stylish-looking—high heels and some kind of nice necklace."

"That's true," Nicholas said. "It hadn't occurred to me that she might be black. . . . What else did your mother say about Anita? Can you remember anything else?"

"Just that she trusts her." It's funny how many things people say that you don't even bother listening to, not knowing someday you'll need them. I looked over at Nicholas. I'd only met him a week ago, but already I felt like I knew him real well. "Maybe you shouldn't be a doctor," I said all of a sudden.

"What?" Nicholas looked distracted, like he'd been thinking about something else.

"Mama says people should do what they truly want to, not just what their parents say they should do. So if you don't really *want* to be a doctor—"

"So what am I going to do? Live off Tara? I've got to do *something*."

"Jean-Claude's going to be a doctor," I said.

"Who's he?"

"My other boyfriend, the one back in France."

Nicholas grinned. "Oh, yeah, I forgot, you've got two of them on the griddle at the same time."

I felt mad. "How about Peter? He has that Danny. I bet anything she's not just his friend. They kiss and everything." I felt bad, remembering how happy I'd felt when he came into my room the night before and how good it felt when he kissed me. Kisses can lead to trouble and foolishness, Mama says.

"What kind of doctor does Jean-Claude want to be?" Nicholas said.

"A—" I tried to remember the word. "The kind that helps people with their mental problems?"

"A psychiatrist?"

"Yeah. He'd be good. He'd talk to them and tell them things to make them feel better."

Then, as Nicholas didn't feel like talking more, I

started pretending that I'd just gotten home from America and was talking to Jean-Claude on the phone, telling him everything that'd happened, making it sound like it had been a lot of exciting adventures and that I hadn't been scared at all. I could almost hear his voice saying, "And then what happened?" He loves to hear people's stories, and he says I tell good ones.

"I think this must be it," Nicholas said. The house he stopped in front of was on a street that had a few other houses, but all around was real country, lots of trees.

We got out and stretched. "God, the air smells terrific," Nicholas said. "It's wonderful."

Mama says country people are hicks. She says that about the peasants who live near Nana's, that they don't know anything and live like animals. We walked up and knocked on the door.

The woman who answered it didn't look like what I expected *or* what Nicholas had said she'd be like either. She was real tiny, not much taller than me, with white skin and short black curly hair. She was wearing a black scoop-necked T-shirt and jeans. As soon as she saw us, she ran right up and hugged me. "Gee, I'm so glad to see you," she said like we knew each other. With Nicholas she just shook his hand. "I'm Anita."

"We're really glad to see you too," Nicholas said. I think he thought she was pretty; I just had that feeling.

Her house was smaller than Tara's. But downstairs there was one big room with a stove in one corner and a big couch and lots of books along one wall. There were books stacked on the floor and some in boxes too. "Excuse the mess," she said. "Duff and I are painting the whole house, and we're right in the middle."

"Is Duff your husband?" Nicholas asked.

She shook her head. "My son . . . I'm not married." After a second she added, "He's adopted."

I wondered how old he was. It would be great if he was my age. "Where is he?"

"He's down at the store. We ran out of paint. He's just started driving so I worry a lot—more than I should, I guess."

Nicholas was still kind of looking her over. "You look awfully young to have a teenage son," he said.

"I'm thirty-three," she said right out. Mama's thirty-three too, but she prefers not to reveal it unless she's in the mood.

"You don't look it," Nicholas said. Boy, if Tara was here, I'll bet anything she'd be jealous. He was sure flirting with Anita Pyne. But it was true, she looked a lot younger than thirty-three—twenty-eight, maybe.

"It's because I'm such a shrimp," she said. "I kept meaning to hit five two, but I never made it."

We sat outside on her porch and Anita brought us lemonade and cookies. She kept looking at me all the time; I felt self-conscious. "You look so grown-up, Ellie!" she said. "I haven't seen you in—well, ten years at least."

I didn't remember *ever* seeing her. "I'm thirteen," I said.

"I know! Gosh, it's hard to believe."

"When did you see her?" Nicholas asked.

Anita frowned. "Let's see . . . Well, I traveled around Europe after I got out of college. Duff and I stopped off in Paris to see Tranquility and Roger." She stopped, as though she thought I'd feel funny at her mentioning my father. "You were just a toddler

80

charging around, getting into everything. He adored you. He kept taking photos of you every second."

I know that part because Mama has a big album of photos from when I was a baby. But since my father died, there haven't been many more. Mama has a camera, but she doesn't use it much.

"What was he like?" Nicholas asked. It was funny he asked that, but I was glad he did because Mama doesn't tell me a whole lot of details about my father.

"Oh, very intense," Anita said. "You know how the French are. Very quick and articulate. You just had the feeling he picked up on everything, even though he didn't know English perfectly." She looked thoughtful. "I wouldn't have picked him for Tranquility if I'd just met him because she can be so—oh, impulsive and quick off the handle herself. But you could see they just had this rapport. It was like watching a very fast Ping-Pong game, the two of them talking, laughing. I envied it."

There was a pause.

"Where do you know Tranquility from?" Nicholas asked.

"School. High school. We were in the same class."

"You both grew up in Pennsylvania?"

Anita nodded. "Tranquility always lived here. Her parents, grandparents, from way back. I just moved here when I was eleven, but we got to be friends right off and—well, that's how it happened." Her face had a funny, sad expression, like she was thinking of a lot of different things at once.

"How what happened?" Nicholas said.

But just then a door slammed and a tall skinny dark boy with a natural-style haircut banged in the doorway. "They didn't have the right kind," he said. "He said they'd get in more later today."

Anita smiled. "Great. We can take it easy for a few hours then. Duff, this is Eliane and Nicholas. My son, Duff."

Chapter 12

Duff is a worse name than Bizou, even. Boy, parents give their kids awful names. I wonder if Anita thought that one up or he just came that way. I had the feeling Duff was shy. He just nodded at us, mumbled something, and went outside.

"Do you want to go out and play, Eliane?" Anita said.

"No, not so much," I said coolly, looking like I didn't know what she was up to. It looked hot out, and he didn't seem at all friendly.

"Go on," Nicholas said, winking at me real quick so Anita couldn't see. "You need some exercise."

"How about you?" I snapped. But I knew what he wanted. He just wanted to have Anita to himself and find out more about her and maybe more about Mama. Grown-ups are so transparent sometimes. But to please him I got up and ambled out.

I couldn't even see Duff, but I went around in the back of the house. There was a smaller house, like a shed, there. I looked into it. There were all these cages with rabbits in them, but not regular rabbits like Nana keeps to cook for dinner. These were big fluffy rabbits with fur. As soon as I came in, they began scampering around, in that nervous way rabbits have. Duff was feeding one of them, some kind of grain. "Are they for eating?" I asked.

"No!" He looked like I was crazy. "These're angora rabbits."

"What're they *for*?"

"Sweaters, stuff like that. . . . Didn't you ever have an angora sweater?"

I shook my head. "From their fur?"

"Yeah. I pull it out, gently so it won't hurt them. Then we sell it to the dealer. . . . Feel this one. She's soft."

I put my hand out and touched the rabbit. You know how soft a kitten is? Well, this was even softer because the fur was so thick. "Can I hold her?"

"They're kind of nervous," Duff said. "Especially with strangers. But we can let her out if you want." He took the big fluffy white rabbit out of her cage and carried her out to the grass in back of the house. For a minute, after he set her down, she just sat there, like she was too scared to move. Her whiskers were twitching. Then all of a sudden she began to hop like crazy all over the yard. She looked like a big powder puff!

"Go, Maisie, go!" Duff said, grinning. "That's the way."

"What if she runs away?"

"They're not that fast. I wouldn't let more than one out at once, though."

The way he talked was a little different from Peter's way of talking, slower. Some words sounded different, like they were stuck together. He got Maisie back and sat with her in his lap, stroking her ears. "You're French?" he said.

"Yeah."

"I took that at school," Duff said shyly. "I can say some things."

"Say something."

He did, but I didn't understand what it was. "That means I'm glad to meet you," he explained.

"I'm glad to meet you," I said slowly in French.

He tried to repeat it, but it came out a little funny. "How come you know English so well?"

"I go to an American school. Lots of my friends are American, and so's my mother."

"So are you going to live here now forever?"

"I don't know."

Then we just sat there. He let me hold the rabbit. She didn't seem to mind too much. "Is that your father?" he said.

I shook my head. "He died when I was three."

"Mine moved away somewhere. I have a grandfather, though."

"I have a grandmother."

I felt sorry for him, being adopted, not even knowing who his real parents were. I wouldn't like that, even if the people who adopted me were nice, like Anita seemed.

"How come your mother didn't come with you?" he asked. He wiped his forehead. He was sweating a lot, even though we were in the shade.

"She's visiting someplace," I said.

"Oh." He looked up at me. "Anita said she'd be

85

coming down here to see us sometime over the summer."

"Maybe later on," I said. I felt uncomfortable, though I don't think he thought I wasn't telling the truth. I kept wondering what Nicholas and Anita were talking about inside. "Does Anita have a boyfriend?" I asked.

Duff shook his head. "She's a teacher. She teaches science."

"Didn't she *ever* have one?"

"She goes out sometimes." He looked annoyed. "But she's not going to get married. She's not the type. She's independent."

"Mine is too. But she still has boyfriends."

"Is he one of them?" Duff pointed to the house.

"Nicholas? No, he just . . . we met him while we were traveling."

It was really hot sitting outside, and even though I was glad to have seen the rabbits, I figured I'd given Nicholas all the time he deserved to put the fix on Anita or find out about Mama or whatever he was up to. "I'm going in," I said. "I'm boiling."

"Could I see the letter?" Nicholas was saying as we walked in.

Anita sighed. "You know, this is awful, but with all this mess with the painting, I just don't know where I put it. I remember what it said pretty well, though."

Duff and I stood there.

"She got a letter from Tranquility about three months ago," Nicholas told me.

"Three months ago! What good would *that* do?"

"Did she sound like she was looking forward to coming over?" Nicholas asked. He had moved his chair real close to Anita's.

86

Anita shrugged. "I think she felt awfully mixed. After she broke with her family, she said she didn't want to ever see them again."

"What was it about?" Nicholas asked. "The break? Was it her getting married? To a foreigner?"

"No, it was before that," Anita said. She was staring off out the window. "It was something that happened when we were in high school."

"What was it?"

Anita looked over at me. "Did Tranquility ever talk about someone named Jimmy?" she asked.

I shook my head.

Anita hesitated. "I don't know if I should talk about it, then. She might still feel funny about it."

"If it would help us find her . . ." Nicholas began. He reached out and touched her arm.

"I don't see how it would," Anita said. "It was so long ago. She hasn't seen him since back then. I know that."

"Tell us about it," Nicholas said, looking at her intently.

"They were in love," Anita said. "That's all. High school romance. Then she got pregnant and had the baby. Her mother would've helped her raise it at home, but she didn't want that. She and her mother didn't get along that well. I guess Tranquility felt bitter about the way Jimmy acted. He was just a kid. He didn't want to settle down. But she really didn't want to either." Anita looked at us. "See. Tranquility didn't want to just be like her parents, living in this one place all her life. She wanted to see things, do things. Not like me. I never left home, really, but Tranquility wanted a different kind of life, something more exciting. I just wanted to settle down."

"You never thought of getting married?"

"Why?" She smiled. "I have Duff for company."

"Yeah, true." Nicholas looked awkward. I think he likes Anita a lot.

"*You're* not married, are you?" she asked him, like she thought he was pretty good too.

He shook his head. I guess he didn't feel like mentioning Tara.

"I like being on my own," Anita said. "Do you think that's bad?"

"No," Nicholas said. "I think it's terrific."

There was a pause. They just sat staring at each other.

"I saw the angora rabbits," I said, just to bring them back to life. Boy, that Jimmy sounded real mean! No wonder Mama never mentioned him. I'm sure more like Mama than Anita. I wouldn't want to settle down that young either, with a baby and all. People are always saying how cute babies are, but how about all the work? I guess I might have one when I'm a whole lot older and have done a bunch of more exciting, interesting things.

Anita smiled. "They're pretty, aren't they? . . . Listen, since it's so hot, why don't we go swimming? By the time we get back, the paint'll be here and we can get at the back porch. Or you can just watch us work, if you're not up to it."

Chapter 13

Anita lent me one of her bathing suits, a bikini. It kind of fit, but you could tell I have some growing to do to fill it out, especially on top. Still, what if she'd been real big? I couldn't have swum at all. So I wasn't that fussy. Nicholas had a suit in the car. It was tight. I didn't expect him to be the kind of man who'd wear that kind of suit. Maybe he just wanted to show his body off to Anita.

"This is what you have to call a water hole," Anita said when we got there.

I didn't mean to be impolite, but she was right. The water was all brown and funny with insects skimming around. But it felt good once you got in. I love swimming. I can go underwater for a long time. Usually I like to open my eyes and see what's going on, but this water was so murky I didn't bother. Duff kept diving in off the deep end and disappearing for a long time. Then suddenly he'd pop up and yell in some place where you didn't expect him to be. He gave me a ride on his shoulders and showed me some big clumps of frog eggs nestled along the bank.

"I like this place," I said. "Do you come here every day?"

"Pretty much. There's a river that's cleaner, but this is more private."

I was beginning to feel all soggy from being in the water so long, but I just didn't want to get out. I knew I'd stay cool for about five minutes and then be all sticky again. I looked up at the shore. Anita had spread out this big towel, and Nicholas was lying on it, looking up at her. She was sitting, leaning against a tree, talking to him.

It's funny that you can actually *see* somebody fall in love with someone else. Mama used to say that maybe there was a real invisible elf like Cupid who shot arrows into people and made them act crazy, for no reason. Anita and Nicholas just kept staring at each other, like they couldn't look at anything else. I like Nicholas, but you can't say he's that handsome. Still, it's nice someone thinks so. I was glad for him.

"I once thought of being a doctor," Anita said as Duff and I climbed on the bank. "But I didn't think I could do all those things like dissect a cadaver."

"That's the fun part," Nicholas said.

I made a face.

"Why're you going, then," Anita asked him, "if you feel so mixed?"

"My grandfather's a surgeon. He wanted my father to be one, but he became an art teacher instead."

"So he's passing the burning torch on to you?"

"Yeah, basically."

She laughed. "Just drop it."

"Drop it?" Nicholas started laughing too in that dopey way people get when they're in love and everything the person they're in love with says sounds funny. I used to be like that with Jean-Claude. Yvonne wouldn't even speak to me for a month. She thought I was acting so bizarre. I'd just look at him and start to giggle. I got over it, though.

"I'm going to be a doctor," Duff said, "like my grandfather."

"Hon, you've got a while to decide," Anita said.

"I did decide," Duff said firmly. "That's what I want to do."

He seemed to be a determined kind of person; I bet he will be one.

We lazed around on the bank for another hour or so. Anita and Nicholas swam around, splashing each other and acting silly. Once Duff looked at me and smiled, and I smiled back. It's funny when grown-ups act like kids.

On the way home we stopped off at a fish store. Duff came back with a big paper bag full of soft-shell crabs. He said he knew how to cook them a special way.

We ate outside, at a long wooden picnic table with newspapers spread out for the crabs. By the time everything got ready, it was getting dark, so Anita brought out these fat yellow candles with glass around them. They put a can of bug spray nearby. There were some bugs, but not too many. "How long can you stay?" she asked Nicholas. They were drinking beer out of big tall glasses with handles.

"I wish I could stay forever," he said dreamily.

"Why don't you?" she said.

He didn't say anything. It's not that I mind Nicholas being in love or whatever he's *in*, but how about me? That's why we came down here, to find Mama, not just to have a good time. But it was funny. Sitting there, I felt so good it was like the thing with Mama never happened, like she just left me to go on a job. In a way I felt almost guilty because I felt so good and relaxed I didn't miss her at all. And in another way I wished she knew, wherever she was, that I could have a good time whether she was there or not. I started thinking how maybe Nicholas and Anita would get married and I could live down here with them. Maybe that would be nice. It's just hard to imagine.

After we had some peaches and cake, Nicholas got his guitar out of the car. I'd seen it there, in a black case, but I'd never heard him play it. He was good! His singing voice wasn't so fine, but he played really well. He sang a whole lot of songs. Anita and Duff knew some and sang along with him. I just hummed and came in on the chorus when I could remember the words.

"I can play a little too," Duff said, "but I'm not as good as that."

He took the guitar and started in playing, but his fingers were stiff. They didn't skim over the strings like Nicholas's had. Duff looked at Anita. "You know who'd like Nicholas's playing, Annie? Grandpa."

Anita smiled. "Yeah, he would, you're right."

"Maybe we should visit him tomorrow and Nick and Ellie can come." To me he said, "Grandpa's in a nursing home. He's eighty. We visit him once a week."

"Aren't those places pretty awful?" Nicholas said.

"This one isn't bad," Anita said. "He was at home

a long time, but he fell a couple of times and fractured his hip."

"He likes visits," Duff said.

"Mentally he's pretty good," Anita said. "He tunes in and out, but . . ."

Nicholas looked at me. "Sure, let's visit him. I'd like that. What do you say, Beez?"

"Okay." I didn't know if I should remind him that we hadn't called the hotel yet today. Usually we call every day just before or after supper. "I'm going to call and check in on Mama," I said.

"Okay, you do that," Nicholas said, not even moving.

I know the number by heart by now, and I guess that man at the desk knows my voice by heart too. I don't even have to say who I am. I gave him Anita's number and told him to have Mama call us there first thing, as soon as she checked in. "I'll do that," he said, but I could tell by his voice he didn't believe she would check in, ever.

When I got back, Duff was sitting there by himself. He said Nicholas and Anita had gone off on a walk. "It looks like there's going to be a storm," he said. "They better not go too far."

It's interesting how with some guys you can like them but not have any desire to kiss them. That's how I felt about Duff. He was friendly and nice, but he didn't turn me on at *all*. I'm glad! Imagine how it would be if you felt that way with everybody of the opposite sex you met! You'd go crazy.

Anita and Nicholas came back not too long after. She said the guest room was too messy for me to sleep in, but I could have the couch in the living room. I didn't ask about where Nicholas would sleep. I knew!

Just about an hour after I got into bed, the storm started. Lots of rain beating down on the house, like people were hitting it with drumsticks. They once showed *The Wizard of Oz* on television, how the house flew clear away into the air because of a certain kind of storm. I hope we aren't in that part of the country.

When I was little, I used to think storms meant someone was mad. One thing I remember about my father was him telling me to go to bed when I was real little, around two or three. I guess I didn't want to; I wanted to stay up and be with him and Mama. Finally he shouted, "Go to bed!" Just as he said "bed," there was a big crack of thunder and lightning. I ran into bed so fast I practically flew! I remember how later he came in and explained how that had just happened; he hadn't *made* it happen.

I wish I remembered more things about him. I remember the way he smelled. He smoked a lot, a kind of French cigarette called Gauloise, and whenever I smell that tobacco smell, I think of him. And I remember his camera and the different lenses that he kept in little cases on a shelf. Once, about a year ago, I saw a man in the park taking a photo of his little girl. I couldn't see his face—he was turned away—but he had dark hair, like my father, and I suddenly got a funny feeling and ran off. . . . And I remember the way he said my name, "Bizou," different from the way Mama does. He'd pucker up his lips in a kiss as he said it. I wish sometimes he'd come back, just for an hour each year so I could explain to him everything that happened to me that year. Mama said if I felt that way I should write him a letter and put it away. But that's pretending. Unless you really believe dead people can see down and know what's going on. I don't think they can.

The storm went on all night, but finally I fell asleep anyway.

Chapter 14

In the morning I woke up, hearing Nicholas whistling as he shaved. He has an electric shaver, like Mama has for her legs. I came by the bathroom, waiting for him to be finished, and he smiled. "Sleep okay?"

"Sure. Did you?"

He just smiled at me in that spaced-out way. "I'm glad you're so good at remembering numbers, kid," he said.

I know *he's* glad because it got him to meet Anita, but it doesn't seem to have brought us any closer to finding Mama. Still it's interesting to know Anita and Mama were friends in school and that this town is where Mama grew up. I can see how she'd like Paris better. There's more going on.

"Next week Grandpa will be eighty," Duff said at breakfast. "We're going to make him a cake."

"He loves chocolate," Anita said. She was wearing a pretty purple dress that came above her knees.

Eighty is really old. Nana, my father's mother, is almost seventy, but she's very spry. She runs her own little house and keeps chickens and rabbits, and she still has a big garden out in back, though she says it's hard for her to stoop down and weed it like she used to. When I visit her, I do a lot of weeding to help her catch up.

We drove up to a building and parked in a big place with a lot of other cars. Nicholas took his guitar with him. I talked with Nana once about where she'd like to go when she gets too old to look after herself. She said nowhere, I should shoot her and bury her out in back so her body would help fertilize her garden, and I should come back and weed, just like I do now. I know she didn't mean that, but coming to this place, I could see what she meant, how it would be depressing to be in a place where everyone was old except the nurses.

Duff's grandfather was a tall man with really dark skin, almost black, all wrinkled, especially near his mouth. He wore glasses and had lots of hair, but his wrinkles gave away how old he was. When we came in, he was sitting in a chair, playing cards with a lady who looked pretty old, too. That lady had a straw hat on and she smiled at us, even though a lot of her teeth seemed to be gone. "It's your grandson," she said excitedly to Duff's grandfather, like he couldn't see.

"I know it's my grandson," Duff's grandfather said in a slow voice. It seemed like it was hard for him to move. He turned his head and looked at all of us. "And a contingent of strangers. A musician and a beautiful little girl. This must be for my birthday."

97

"Your birthday's not till next week, sweetie," Anita said.

"Oh, we can start celebrating right now," Duff's grandfather said. He smiled at me. "Can't start celebrating too early, can you, miss? . . . What's her name, Annie?"

"Eliane," Anita said.

I put out my hand to shake his. "Hi," I said.

"Are you one of my presents?" he said.

I laughed. "I'm just visiting."

"Aha! And who's the lucky fellow you're visiting?"

"You."

"Me?" He looked at the lady in the straw hat. "I told you I was lucky today, Thelma."

"He gets more visitors than anyone," Thelma grumbled. "It's not fair."

"Not much that's fair in life, is there now?" he said. He looked up at Nicholas. "You're the entertainer, I suppose. Come to play me some nice songs. Are you as good as my grandson here?"

"He's good, Grandpa," Duff said. "He's excellent."

"Excellent," Duff's grandfather said slowly. "Well, we can't have too much excellence. It's in short supply these days." He shook hands with Nicholas. "I'm Beal Roberts, and you—"

"Nicholas Berend," Nicholas said.

"Nicholas is a good name," Mr. Roberts said. "I used to have a best friend named Nicholas. All right, Mr. Nicholas, we're ready to be entertained. Are you ready, Thelma?"

"I sure am," she said, looking all excited.

I thought Nicholas might be nervous, playing for an

audience that way. A lot of old people in different parts of the room stopped what they were doing to hear him. But he wasn't nervous. He sat down and played, just like he had the night before. But he kept looking over at Anita and smiling in that goofy way, especially when he sang this one melty kind of love song called "Greensleeves."

When he stopped, Mr. Roberts clapped. "Fine!" he said. "That was truly fine. You must have a wide audience for your music, Mr. Nicholas."

"Not *too* wide," Nicholas said, smiling.

"Someday you will. You give it time. Mustn't rush things."

"I won't," Nicholas said. "I try not to, anyway."

Then Mr. Roberts looked at me. "What do *you* do?" he asked.

"I go to school," I said.

"Which school do you go to around here?"

"It's in Paris," I said. "Paris, *France*."

Mr. Roberts smiled at me again. "You came all the way from Paris, France, to pay me a visit?" he said. "Think of that."

I hadn't exactly come all the way just to see *him* because I didn't even know about him. But I didn't deny it. He put out his hand and touched my cheek. "Beautiful," he said, but in a funny, sad way.

There was a pause.

"Eliane is Tranquility's little girl," Anita said softly.

Mr. Roberts kept staring at me so hard it made me nervous. "Tranquility's girl?" he said.

She nodded.

"Well," he said. "That's about the best birthday present I can think of."

99

I didn't know what to say. But he was staring at me so I just stood there.

"Where's your mama?" Mr. Roberts said. "Did she come with you?"

"She's off on a trip," I said.

"Yes," he said. Then he added, "You look like her. Your eyes."

"Thank you," I said, because I think he meant it as a compliment.

"And how do you like your life in Paris, France?" Mr. Roberts said.

"I like it."

"You don't want to come back and settle here, in this country?"

"Maybe for college." I hesitated. "Mama says there's a lot of prejudice here against black people."

"That's true," Mr. Roberts said. "I can't deny that." He stared at me in that intent way again. "And you don't encounter any of that in that country you chose to live in?"

"Not so much."

"Well, people make different choices and then they have to live with them. Your mama's happy with her life there, I suppose?"

I nodded.

"She marry again?"

I wondered how he knew so much about Mama. "No, but she has boyfriends sometimes. She's an independent woman."

Mr. Roberts smiled. "Yes, she always was that, for sure." He touched my arm. "You tell your mama if she ever cares to, to come on down here and visit. We like independent ladies down here, don't we, Thelma?"

Thelma nodded. "*He* does. . . . Not all of them."

At that moment a nurse came over and said, "I believe it's getting on to lunchtime." To Anita she said, "You'll come back later in the week for his real birthday?"

"Of course."

"I'm making you a cake, Grandpa," Duff said. "Three layers."

"All chocolate?" Mr. Roberts said. "Promise?"

"All chocolate, icing and everything."

Mr. Roberts smiled at me. "I'm a chocolate fiend. You have to watch your chocolate when I'm nearby. Especially bittersweet."

"Mama likes bittersweet," I said.

Just as we were about to leave, Mr. Roberts grabbed hold of me and hugged me real hard. "You're the best present," he whispered. "The best."

I wondered what he meant.

Chapter 15

"**H**e's a great old guy," Nicholas said when we were outside again. "I hope I'll be like that at eighty, if I ever get there."

"You will," Anita said, smiling up at him, taking his hand and interlocking her fingers with his.

"What happened to his wife?"

"She died about fifteen years ago. Usually it's the husbands that go first, but she hadn't been too well for a long while."

I sat in the back of the car as we drove home, looking out at the kids my age passing on the streets, thinking: This is Mama's home town. She must've looked in this window, walked around this corner. You'd think she'd be curious to see how it'd changed, if anything was new or different. "How come he knew so much about Mama?" I asked suddenly.

There was a pause.

I thought maybe Anita didn't hear me, but just as I was about to repeat the question, she said, "He's her father."

"You mean he's *my* grandpa too?" I said, looking at Duff, who looked just as surprised as me.

"Annie, how can he be?" Duff said. "He can't be her grandpa *and* mine too."

"Yes, he can. . . . Look, wait till we get home. I'll explain it then."

Duff and I looked at each other. We both pulled away and sat as far apart as we could. Was he my brother or what? It didn't seem like something anyone would make up, but it didn't make much sense either.

We all got out of the car and went into the living room. There was a painty smell from the new can of paint Duff had opened that morning. We'd already started on the front hall. Anita sat cross-legged on the floor. "Remember Jimmy, who I told you about yesterday?" she asked.

"Mama's high school sweetheart?" I did remember, though Mama had never mentioned him at all, not even once.

"Jimmy was your father, Duff," Anita said to him. "Only he—he just didn't dig being a father at seventeen or whatever. I can't blame him much. No more than Tranquility dug the idea of being a mother. But you know how it is. Boys can just take off, wash their hands of the whole thing. Girls get stuck."

"So did Mama give her baby to you?" I asked.

"No, it didn't work that way exactly. First Lia, your grandmother, offered to take him. But the doctor said no, absolutely not. She had a bad heart. That's why she had only one child. Tranquility was an only child of older parents, and—you know how it is—hovered over quite a bit. I don't think she would've been too happy over her mother raising her baby anyway. But the doctor said no way, Lia just couldn't manage it. So I said I'd take the baby." Anita smiled at Duff. "It was crazy, in a way. But I'd always wanted a baby brother. My mother only had me just like Tranquility's mother only had her but for different reasons. My father cleared out when I was little and she never remarried. I thought my mother would hit the ceiling when I said that was what I wanted to do, but she said if I did it, it was my decision. She wasn't quitting her job to stay home and help me. She wanted to make sure I knew, really knew, what I was getting into. Of course I didn't!"

Duff had a real peculiar expression. "How come you never told me any of this? You said I came from that agency."

Anita frowned. "I guess I was afraid if you knew you had a real mother out there, someone we both knew, you might just up and leave someday, decide you liked her better than me. I'm still scared of that!" She laughed nervously.

"If I never see her, how could I do that?" Duff asked.

"Oh, you'll see her," Anita said. "She'll turn up."

"Did you do it because Mama was your best friend?" I said.

"Yeah, partly. . . . See, boys, men never liked me all that much then. I thought maybe I'd never have a chance again. And I wasn't sure I wanted to be married, even if someone would have me. So this way I thought I'd get it all done right at the beginning. Maybe it gave me an excuse, in a way. I had a family built in."

"I don't think it was an excuse," Nicholas said.

"You never know," Anita said. "Even if it's you, it's so hard to know what your motives really are." She looked at Duff and then back at Nicholas. "I never regretted it, that's all I know. It was the right thing to do."

I kept thinking back on the old man in the nursing home and that way he kept staring at me and the way he'd touched my cheeks so softly, saying, "Beautiful." "I thought Tranquility didn't get along with her family," I said.

"Oh, it was her mother mostly. Beal adored her. He still does. Every time we visit, that's all he wants to know: Did I hear from her? Any letters? It's pathetic almost. But I didn't tell him she might be over this summer because I wasn't sure if she'd come and I didn't know if she'd want to see him if she did come."

"Why is she still mad at him," I asked, "if her mother died?"

"Oh, I think it worked itself into a whole tangled web of things," Anita said, "the way things do. It seemed to Beal she was abandoning everything by going to live in Paris—them, her son, her country. He didn't like the idea of her marrying a white man, especially a Frenchman, thought their children would suffer. And then Beal had such high expectations for Tranquility. He had his heart set on her being a doctor, and he can be pretty stiff-backed." She reached out and squeezed my hand. "I'm glad you went to see him, Ellie. I could tell how glad he was."

It's funny, all of a sudden, at thirteen, I have a grandfather and a brother, or a half brother, anyway. I wonder how Nana and Mr. Roberts would get on. She's stiff-backed too, but in a different way.

Suddenly Duff got up. "Boy, this is crazy," he said angrily. "I bet you're making the whole thing up!" He slammed on out of the house.

"Why would I do that?" Anita asked gently. But he was gone.

She bent over and started to cry. "That was stupid," she wailed. "I shouldn't have done it."

Nicholas went over and put his arms around her. "No, it's good," he said. "He's better off knowing."

"Why? It just stirs things up. I did mean to tell him someday, when he was twenty or so, really grown up. What if he leaves and never comes back?"

"Don't be silly, Annie," Nicholas said. "He's just upset."

It made me feel bad, to two of them sitting there, comforting each *other*. No one even seemed to care about me! I walked to the door but Nicholas was patting Anita on the back and saying how she ought to have something cool to drink or lie down. I felt *really* fed up, I can tell you.

I went on back outside. Duff wasn't anywhere around. He must've taken the car, because it wasn't there. Well, at least he's old enough so if he wants to go off, he can. I can't drive, I don't have any money. What can I do? I went in to look at the rabbits. I thought of taking one out, but what if they run off? I guess Anita and Duff must make some money out of them. It smelled funny in the rabbit house, stuffy.

I went outside. I thought of that scene in *The Wizard of Oz* where Dorothy clicks her heels together and thinks she's home again and she is. Why can't it be like that in real life? While I was standing there, Duff walked over. I don't know where he'd been, but he went over to the car. "Let's go," he said.

"Where?"

"Just for a drive."

"Okay." I jumped in next to him, and we went off down the road. "Where're we going?"

"Where do you want to go?"

"Paris, France."

He made a face. "Sorry, sis, this vehicle barely makes it over land. I don't think it would get too far on water."

"I *hate* this town!" I said suddenly. "How can you live here?"

"What's wrong with it?"

"It's so small. Nothing happening. I don't blame Mama. I'd go *crazy* here."

"I like it," he said defensively. "You and your mama sound pretty snobbish. What's so great about Paris, France?"

Actually, there are lots of things about France I don't like, but I said, "I guess I just feel at home there."

Duff didn't say anything. "I must be dumb," he said, half to himself.

"About what?"

"All that stuff Anita told us about Grandpa. I never picked up on *any* of that. I remember how he used to ask about your mama a whole lot, but I never thought about it much."

"Do you mind that I'm your sister?" I asked.

"You're my *half* sister."

Talk about snobbish! "Okay, your *half* sister."

"I can handle it."

"Thanks a lot."

"It might be different if you were around all the time. I don't know how I'd dig that. Joey, my best friend, he has two sisters, and they're always fussing around in the bathroom and giggling over dumb things. I couldn't take that."

"That's prejudiced," I said. "*I* don't do that. . . . Don't you even have a girl friend or anything?"

"No! Why should I?"

"You're backward," I told him. "What are you—fifteen?"

"Sixteen. And I'm not backward, pip-squeak. I just don't like girls. None of the ones around here anyway."

"I have *two* boyfriends," I told him.

"Sure."

"I do. . . . One's French and one's American."

"What I don't like," Duff said, like he didn't care about boyfriends or girl friends, "is her keeping secrets like that. She's always saying how everything ought to be open."

"Yeah, I know. . . . Mama never told *me* anything about it either."

"What we ought to do—we ought to just go off, give them a real scare. . . . Only I don't have enough gas."

I thought of how scared Mama got me by going off. That idea didn't appeal to me much. "Let's go back," I said.

Duff seemed to be just concentrating on the driving. But then he said, "I know where we'll go."

"Where?"

"To see Grandpa. I want to find out if Annie told us the truth."

"She couldn't have made it up."

"Let's ask him. He'll tell us."

Chapter 16

The nurse at the home Grandpa was in said he was resting and we should come back later.

"When?" Duff asked.

"Three o'clock should be good."

I didn't want to say anything, but I felt starving and faint, I was so hungry. "I want to have lunch," I said.

"Okay, I don't have much money, though," Duff said. He took me into this drugstore and we had Cokes and hot dogs.

"I like your grandfather," I said.

"We used to do a lot together," Duff boasted, "fishing, going on trips. We went off to New Orleans once and stayed at a fancy hotel with a balcony. But then he started getting weaker."

I wondered if Duff minded the idea of sharing his grandfather with me. "Do you think he'll live a long time?"

"Oh, sure. Maybe to a hundred."

When we got to the home, Mr. Roberts was up. He was sitting outside in a patch of shade, doing some kind of embroidery on a piece of canvas. It was a pattern of leaves and flowers. "Back again?" he asked, but I could tell he was glad to see us.

"There's something we want to ask you about," Duff said, standing up straight.

Mr. Roberts put down his embroidery. "Ask away."

Duff told him all that Anita had described to us. "Is that all true?" he demanded.

"It sounds true to me," Mr. Roberts said.

"What do you mean—it 'sounds' true?" Duff said angrily. "Do we have the same mother or not?"

"It looks like you do," Mr. Roberts said. "Why? Don't you like it? I'd be delighted to have this young lady for my sister any day. Want to trade her?"

We just stood there, looking at him. He seemed so calm about everything. "They should have told us," I said. "That's what we're mad about. They never told us anything."

Mr. Roberts looked at me keenly. "Your mama never told you anything about me or her mother?"

I shook my head.

He cleared his throat. "Well, maybe it was my fault, just a little. I could be pigheaded back then. She seemed so young to be rushing off like that, not even trying college. You know, in this country having a college education is very important for a black person. It shouldn't be like that, but it is. And here we had the money, Tranquility had good school grades. She could have gotten in anywhere. Then to throw it all away to be a model!" He looked disgusted.

"She liked traveling," I told him. It's funny. Even

110

though I felt mad at Mama for running off and for keeping all this stuff to herself, still when someone else started attacking her, I felt like defending her.

"What's *that* got to do with it?" he grumbled. "No one stopped her from traveling. She could have gone around the world! She could've gotten some training, established herself in a real profession."

"I'm going to be a photographer," I said.

"Good," he said. "You do that. . . . No, Tranquility could've been so many things. She'd have made a fine doctor. I told her that. She's good with people. It all seemed like such a waste."

"It isn't," I said. "She does things, she studies. She's not wasting her life."

"She could have been a teacher, like *your* mama," Mr. Roberts said, like he hadn't even heard me, turning to Duff. "*That's* a fine profession. Your grandmother was a teacher when I met her."

"What's so great about being a teacher?" Duff said. "Anyway, Annie's not my mother. She's just the person who raised me."

Mr. Roberts looked mad. "Just the person who raised you, huh? None of that counts? You kids! Anita's been a good mother to you. Tranquility's lucky she had a friend like that. Abandoning her own child to end up in some foreign country married to a white man!" He looked back at me. "Don't misunderstand me, Miss Eliane. Your mama's a fine person, in spite of all this. She's had a hard time, a widow without her folks nearby. That isn't easy."

I couldn't figure out *whose* side he was on! He seemed to keep changing back and forth. I didn't say anything; neither did Duff. Then Duff said in a quieter voice, "We know they did a good job, Grandpa. We just got mad that they didn't tell us anything."

"They had their reasons," Mr. Roberts said. His voice kept getting lower, like he was running out of steam. "What would the point have been? Telling you when you were little? You wouldn't have understood. Maybe you don't understand now."

"We do," I said. "We understand."

"Good." Suddenly he smiled. "Well, this is certainly a special day for me. Two visits in one day. Maybe we need more upsets and revelations, if that's what it takes to get me all this company. . . . How'd you *get* here anyway?"

"I'm learning to drive," Duff said.

"He's good," I said. "Only the road was a little bumpy."

Mr. Roberts laughed. "Well, you haven't done so badly, Miss Eliane, picking a brother out at thirteen. You could have done worse."

"Thanks," Duff said ironically.

"How do you like having me as a grandpa?" he said. "Do I pass muster?"

I nodded. "I like you, Mr. Roberts."

"Oh, we're going to be formal, are we? How about just Grandpa. Try that on for size."

"Grandpa," I echoed.

"That's more like it."

Then the nurse came over. "Okay, Mr. Roberts, I think we better let these young folks go on home. We don't want to tire you out."

"Who's tired?" Grandpa said. "Not me."

"We'll see you on your birthday," Duff said. "You be good, okay?"

"I'm always good." Grandpa sighed. "Good as

gold. I wish your grandmother were around to appreciate it. No point in a show without an audience."

Outside we got into the car. It was hot! Duff had forgotten and parked it right in the blazing sun. We opened all the windows so we could get the breezes going home.

When we got there, Anita and Nicholas came rushing out, asking where we'd been. We told them. They didn't seem mad, like I expected. All Anita said was, "I hope this wasn't too much excitement for him, all in one day."

"He said he likes excitement," Duff said. "He told me once things are too dull around there. Nothing to do but read and play cards and watch TV."

"I wish I could take him to Paris," I said, "show him all the sights."

"Take me!" Duff said.

"Okay." I looked at Anita. "Could he come, for a visit?"

She had a troubled expression. "Maybe someday," she said, "if everything works out."

Chapter 17

The next day Nicholas said he had to leave. "I've got to find a place to stay," he said. "When that's all settled, I'll come back down, if there's time before classes start."

"We'll be okay," Anita said. "School'll start pretty soon too. I'll be busy again."

They both acted kind of sad and awkward, like they didn't exactly know where things stood. While they were hugging and kissing good-bye, I went outside. I felt really bad about Nicholas going away. I knew he had to, but I'd been sure he'd stay with me till Mama turned up. Or that he'd take me with him. What was I going to do now? Live here with Duff and Anita in this little bitty hick town? They're nice people, but I don't want to do that.

"So, Beez," Nicholas said. We were by ourselves out in back. "I wish you could come with me."

"I do too," I said. After a second I asked, "Why can't I?"

He sighed. "I just can't swing it. I'll be studying around the clock. I don't have any money saved. You need a regular home, a school."

"I don't like it here," I said.

"Anita's a wonderful person," he said. "She'll take good care of you."

"Yeah," I said. I guess that's true, but I didn't like the idea of it, not at all. And I hated how he wasn't even talking about Mama coming back, like he had given up on the idea of it happening. "Thanks for taking me around," I said, because Mama says you should always try to be polite, no matter how you're feeling.

He hugged me close for a long time. "I'll call tonight," he said, looking right at me.

"Okay."

But after Nicholas left, I felt real empty and sad. I took a long walk by myself down the road, even though I knew I should've been helping Duff and Anita finish the painting. Everything was all dusty and dry. Anita said it hadn't rained for several weeks except for that lightning storm the other night. I wish it was possible to walk clear around the world, in a big circle, till finally you came to where you started. But this road just went on and on, so eventually I turned and came back.

Anita and Duff tried to be nice to me. They told me how good the local school was and how I'd be better at French than anybody else, even the teacher. So what? I think maybe if Mama doesn't show up by Monday, I'll write Nana and ask her if I can come live with her. Like she says, she still has plenty of pep left in her.

And I could be a real help to her around her farm. I don't eat so much, and she grows everything anyway. She doesn't live too far from Paris, so every now and then I'll take the bus and go back to visit all my friends.

"I'll take you around and show you the school tomorrow," Duff said.

He did. I figured I didn't have to tell him my plans for not going there. It was just a long brick building, not too high. All the buildings seem so flat and kind of ugly to me here. "That part down there," he said. "That's the gym. We have a swimming pool and everything. I'm on the team."

We got out and walked around. Some lady saw us and waved. "Hi there, Duff," she said. "Who's your friend?" It's a good thing Mama wasn't there. She would have said that lady looked like she'd been crumpled up in a ball and stuffed under the bed all night. Nothing she had on matched! She was even wearing red sneakers, and she was old.

"This is my sister," he said. "Ellie, this is Miss O'Malley—she's my French teacher."

"I'm French," I said, and in French I said, "I'm just here visiting."

"Maybe you'll come to our school," Miss O'Malley said. "What grade are you in?"

"I'm thirteen."

"I could use a helper," Miss O'Malley said. "My French is getting a little rusty. I haven't been there for ten years. It's a wonderful country! Did you spend much time there?"

"She's *from* there," Duff said impatiently. "She *lives* there."

"Oh," Miss O'Malley said. "Lucky you. I plan to get back one of these days, but you know how it is."

When Duff and I were in the car again, he grinned. "So how'd you like it?"

"It's nice," I said, trying to sound enthusiastic. I looked up at him. "Hey, will you teach me to drive?"

"I can't," he said. "You're too young."

"Mama said *she* learned when she was thirteen. Her father took her out and taught her when no one was watching."

"If I did that, I could lose my license or something," he said.

I kept thinking how, if I knew how to drive, I could just drive my way out of this place, keep on going till I hit New York, and then hop on a plane to Paris. I bet I could learn too. I've been watching Duff and it doesn't look that hard.

Nicholas called a few nights later. He told us he got a room to stay in.

"Is it nice?" Anita said. I was listening on the kitchen phone.

"Pretty small, but right near where most of my classes are."

"When do they start?"

"Day after tomorrow."

There was a pause.

"Well, we all miss you," Anita said. "A lot."

"Yeah," I said.

"I miss you too," Nicholas said. "I wish I could come down again, but it looks like I'll be tied up here for a while anyway."

I talked to Nicholas alone for a while. I told him how we'd gone to see the school.

"So you're getting used to life there?" he said.

"No, not really."

"You'll get used to it, hon."

117

"No, I won't! I won't *ever* get used to it." I hung up without even saying good-bye. That was mean. It's not Nicholas's fault. In a week or so school will start down here. Anita's talking about taking me shopping for new clothes—jeans and sneakers, more American-looking clothes. I have American jeans already, and I don't like sneakers. I like the clothes I have. She says I can have the little room upstairs under the eaves. She used to use it to do her work in, but she can move her desk into the living room.

I keep thinking of my room at home. It isn't that big, but it has a beautiful view. When I look out my window, I can see the roofs of lots of houses. Mama said we're real lucky to have such a good view and enough room. Paris is getting so crowded it's hard to find a place to stay. I thought of that couple we rented our place to. It was a man and a woman, English people who had to be there just a month. They had a dog and were worried Mama might object, but she said no, it was fine. "My husband was allergic to dogs," Mama said, "but I don't mind them at all."

The next afternoon Anita said she and Duff were going to have a picnic outside, under this big old tree in the field behind their house. There's a cold stream running nearby, and you can put cans of Coke and ginger ale in it to keep them cold. Duff showed me how. But I didn't feel hungry that much. I told them I was going to stay back and read and maybe join them later.

After they left, I went out on the porch. Even though we finished up the painting almost a week ago, and we leave all the windows open day and night, there's still a painty smell. I don't mind it, but Anita says she hopes it'll go away soon. I lay in the hammock, moving it back and forth with my foot. I knew maybe I should've gone on the picnic with them, but I didn't feel in the mood. Sometimes Anita is so cheerful I can't stand it.

The phone rang. I let it ring a few times and then got up to answer it. "Hello?" I said.

"Bizou? Honey? It's me, it's Mama."

This is crazy, but I got so scared hearing Mama's voice that I put the phone back on the hook. Then I ran outside and started to cry. I don't know what I was crying about. Here I'd been waiting to hear from her, thinking about her every day, but when I heard her voice, something happened inside me. Then the phone started ringing again. But instead of answering it, I ran across the field to where Duff and Anita were. I screamed, "It's Mama, it's Mama!" as loud as I could till I got to where they were.

Anita jumped up. "Where?" she said.

I couldn't speak, I was still crying, so I just ran with them back to the house. My side ached from running so hard, but I ran all the way. Duff got there first.

"Where is she?" he said.

Both he and Anita looked at me.

"She's not here," I said. I tried to explain, but instead I started crying again.

"We know she's not here," Duff said, but Anita interrupted him with, "Hush. Can't you see she's upset? Where did you see her, Ellie? Tell us. Did you see her?"

Then the phone started to ring again, and Anita went to answer it.

Chapter 18

I don't remember what Anita and Mama said on the phone. I put my hands over my ears and sat there, not wanting to hear. After a while Anita came out and pulled one of my hands away. "She wants to speak to you," she said. "Come on, Ellie."

"No," I said. "I won't." I'm never going to speak to Mama again, ever, and I don't care what she says or what explanations she has for running off.

Anita just stood there and looked at me. "Okay," she said quietly.

When she came back, she sat down in a chair near me. "She'll be here tonight," she said, "around dinnertime."

I didn't say anything.

"Don't you want to know where she's been?"

"No."

Anita put her hand on my shoulder. "Honey, your

mother's going to feel very bad if you don't say anything to her when she comes here. She's been through a hard time."

"I don't care." I didn't. I didn't want to hear anything about it—how she was raped or murdered or *anything*. I thought maybe when Mama came I wouldn't even be there. Maybe I'd hide in the car or someplace where they couldn't find me. But in the end I just lay there on my bed all afternoon, not even noticing the time going by, just staring at the ceiling.

When the car pulled up, I watched from the window. I saw Mama get out. It was a cab that let her off and then drove away again. She looked fine, in her red dress with her high heels and her sunglasses, just like nothing had happened. She and Anita hugged each other for a long time. Then I heard Mama ask, "Where's Bizou?"

"She hasn't been feeling too well," Anita said. "She's a little run-down."

"Where is she?"

"I think she's upstairs, resting."

My heart starting thumping as I heard them coming upstairs. I didn't want them to find me. For a second I thought of hiding in the closet, but I knew they'd look in there. Then I got an idea. The window was half open and I pushed it up the rest of the way and crawled through onto the roof. They won't find me there, I bet.

I heard them come into the room. Anita said, "That's funny. I was sure she was up here, reading. I didn't hear her come down."

Then the two of them began calling, "Bizou! Bizou!" They went out of the room and back downstairs again. I couldn't hear them downstairs, but I knew they were probably asking Duff if he'd seen me and he was saying no. I sat all scrunched up, glad they couldn't find me. Then I heard the footsteps coming up the stairs again. This time it was all three of them.

"She's got to be somewhere," Anita was saying.

"I'll find her," Duff said.

You know something? He marched right over to the window and looked out to where I was sitting, on the roof. "What're you doing out there?" he said, like he thought I was crazy.

"I'm not coming in," I said.

Anita and Mama came to the window too. "Honey, what're you *doing* out there?" Mama said, sounding alarmed.

I moved away from them. I wouldn't even answer. I just looked out in the opposite direction, my back to them.

"Well, I'm going to get her," Duff said.

"You be careful," Anita said. "I don't want both of you out there. I don't want you getting hurt. Bizou, come back in, honey. Okay?"

"She won't come unless I get her," Duff said. I heard him push the window way open again; it had slid back down after I came out. He started crawling over the roof to where I was. I got so scared I stood up and ran to the edge of the roof. Then I jumped off!

At first I didn't think I was hurt that much, but when I tried to get up, I couldn't move. It was like my whole leg had fallen off. All three of them came running down, yelling and carrying on.

"What'd you do that for?" Duff said angrily. "You crazy?"

"Duff, hush," Anita said. "How do you feel?"

Mama came over and put her arms around me. She was crying. "Honey, why'd you do that?"

"Why'd you run off?" I said, and then I started hurting so bad I couldn't even talk. I felt really dizzy and fell back on the ground. I don't even remember much what they said after that. I know Duff picked me up and carried me into the car and we all drove to the hospital.

It must've taken a long time, but it seemed really quick. Some doctor came and felt my leg and said it was broken and that he'd take care of it. I think he gave me a shot of something because the dizzy feeling got a whole lot worse, and when I woke up there I was lying there with a big cast on my leg. No one was in the room with me but Mama.

"How're you feeling?" she asked quietly.

"I don't know."

She came over and sat right near where I was. "I feel bad," I said. "It hurts."

Instead of saying I shouldn't have jumped that way, Mama just sighed. "I'm sorry, Beez . . . I truly am."

"So why did you do it?"

"I can't explain the whole thing. It was wrong, I know that. But I just felt like I couldn't handle it, our being here, what I'd done with my life, seeing Daddy again, the way they treat black people here. It was like everything just *came* at me."

"Where'd you go?"

She looked at me. "I just went off by myself. I—"

"Why didn't you tell us where?"

"It was stupid! I said that."

I managed to sit halfway up and glare right into her eyes. "Don't you ever do that again," I said. "Ever. I don't care how you feel."

"Someday, when you're older, you'll understand," Mama said in a tired voice.

"No, I won't!" I said. "I won't *ever* understand."

"I missed you a whole lot."

I guess she wanted me to say how I missed her, but I wouldn't. "We had a lot of fun," I said, wanting to spite her. "I like Nicholas."

"I liked him too," Mama said. "He's a good person."

"Does he know you're back?"

"No, I'll call him tonight."

"He isn't used to dealing with kids," I said. "You put him to a whole lot of trouble."

"I know!" Mama said. "Let up, honey, okay? I know I did a wrong thing. But I'm back. I came back, didn't I?"

That's true. I wonder if she ever thought of not coming back at all. I just stared at her. She didn't look any different. You couldn't tell, looking at her, that anything was wrong. It's funny how you can live with someone your whole life and still don't know everything about them. Maybe even if you're married to them, you don't.

"I met Grandpa," I said.

"How'd you like him?"

"I do. I hope Duff doesn't mind sharing him with me."

"Oh, I don't think he'd mind," Mama said in more like her old easy, relaxed way.

That night I went to sleep early. When I was alone in the room, I looked out the window. I thought of how I'd jumped off the roof of Anita's house. I hope that doesn't show I'm a crazy person. I don't think so. Mama says sometimes you find yourself doing things you never expected, and not all those unexpected things are wonderful. That's true.

The first night I got back from the hospital I ate downstairs with everyone. They said I could have a tray in bed, but I didn't feel sick. It was just awkward, trying to figure out how to move around with crutches on.

"I told Beal you were here," Anita said to Mama. "He's so excited to see you he's ready to burst."

Mama'd been just picking around at her food. "I don't know," she said. "I just feel so ashamed, even to see him."

"Don't be silly," Anita said. "What did you do that was so wrong?"

"Everything!" Mama said. "My whole life. Running from place to place, like a chicken with its head cut off. He was right. I should've just stayed here and been a doctor and led a regular orderly life, like he wanted me to."

Anita smiled. "You'd have gone crazy, though."

Mama smiled back. "I know."

Duff had been staring at her the whole time, all through supper, in a way that would've made me nervous. "How come you didn't ever visit us?" he said suddenly, sounding angry. "Or write or *anything*?"

Mama looked confused. "I know, I should've," she said softly. She reached out to touch him. "I wanted to."

"If you wanted to, why didn't you?"

"It didn't seem fair. I mean, I couldn't hack the responsibility back then, and to just be sending postcards from Paris, 'Hi, folks, here I am'—it seemed better to just make a clean break."

"For you, maybe." He sounded really bitter.

Mama was staring at him in this almost pleading way. "I *thought* of you a lot, Duff. Anita sent me pictures. I kept them all in a box and at night I'd take them out to look at them."

"So is that all you're going to do from now on?"

"What do—what do you want me to do?" I've hardly ever seen Mama so flustered.

"If you're my mother, you ought to start acting like one. Or else get on out and forget us and never come back."

Mama didn't say anything. She was just looking down at her plate. I thought maybe she was going to cry. I also thought Duff was acting kind of mean, though I could see how he felt.

"*I'm* your mother," Anita said sharply. "And don't you talk like that to Tranquility! Can't you see she's tired and has been through a lot?"

"You're both just liars," he said. "You never told me the truth about anything."

Anita jumped to her feet and grabbed him. "So what do you wish we'd done? Dumped you at some agency like most teenage mothers do? So you could bum around from foster home to foster home? You haven't had such a bad deal. Okay, so you think neither of us is the world's greatest mother. Who is, tell me that?"

He shrugged.

Mama sighed. "He's right, though. Maybe we should've—"

"Okay, so we should've done lots of things!" Anita burst out. "But we did our best. And I feel proud of what *I* did!"

126

"You should," Mama said wearily. "He's such a fine-looking boy."

"That's just genes," I commented. They were all ignoring my presence, like I wasn't even there.

"Where's my father?" Duff went on. I knew the mood he was in because I can get like that too, stubborn and refusing to let up. "I don't even know where he is. Maybe he'd like to see me."

There was a pause. Mama and Anita looked at each other.

"I guess we could try to locate him," Mama said.

"Sure," Anita said wryly. "Since evidently *mothers* don't make a heck of a lot of difference around here."

"I didn't say that," Duff said.

"Most people only have one mother, and you've got two, so stop bitching," I said. Maybe that wasn't nice, but he was sure acting nasty. "And I don't have a father, either, so don't think you're the only one in the world. Lots of people don't! Lots of people have mothers and fathers they hate! Who treat them mean and starve them and—" I stopped because I'd run out of breath.

Duff laughed. "Cat found her tongue."

"I never lost it," I snapped back.

But he was smiling. "I have a sister just one day and *she* starts jumping off roofs—"

"I wouldn't have if you hadn't come out at me," I said defensively. "I just—"

"Kids, settle down, will you?" Anita said. She got up and poured some coffee. "Tranquility and I'd like to talk in peace if you don't mind. Go play Monopoly or something."

"I gave my set away," Duff said.

"So just tickle each other's toes and stay out of mischief, okay?"

Duff and I looked at each other and smiled. In the end we found another game, Risk, and it was just as good. I won, not because I was cheating. I'm just good at games. It must be genes or something.

Chapter 19

The next day we went to the nursing home for Grandpa's eightieth birthday. I could tell Mama was nervous about seeing him. She kept fussing with herself in front of the mirror, like she was going on some big date. I didn't want to tell her, but she looked terrific just like she was, a lot prettier and more stylish than anyone in the State of Pennsylvania, that's for sure.

"He never liked me to fuss about my looks," she said, putting her earrings on. "He said brains were more important."

"You can't help being pretty," I consoled her.

"No, but he's right. I didn't give my brains a chance. I put them on the back burner."

"You can still do something with them," I said. "You're not *that* old."

Mama laughed. "Thanks, Beez."

I told her I thought maybe Anita and Nicholas were in love with each other. "I'm glad," Mama said. "Anita's had a hard time here. I don't mean with Duff. I think he's been good for her. But she's always been so—strong-minded, and men don't always like that."

"*You're* strong-minded," I reminded her.

"Yeah, but I—I flirt around a lot more than she does. She's just herself all the time, the same with men as with women. I respect it, but it doesn't always get you a lot of boyfriends."

"Maybe she didn't want any," I suggested.

"Maybe. Anyhow, I'm glad. Nicholas is a sweetie."

"I thought maybe you wanted him for yourself," I said.

"Nicholas? Hon, he's just a baby."

"You said age doesn't matter."

"Yeah, but he's so—" She gestured, looking for the right word. "He has to grow up a little. I raised one kid. That's enough."

I couldn't help needling her a little. "I guess you're pretty proud of me," I said, "how I handled myself when you took off, how I kept my cool, found Anita just from her zip code."

Mama hugged me. "I am. That you get from your father. He didn't fly apart in a crisis. The French are like that. They seem so emotional and what-have-you, but deep down they get through. They're sensible." For Mama "sensible" is a big compliment. She doesn't like people who don't use their heads.

At the nursing home, we gave the cake to the nurse, who said she'd bring it in later. It was big and flat, all covered with chocolate. We'd put eighty candles on it! I had to hobble in, wearing my crutches. Mama went first. She walked right over to Grandpa like she wasn't nervous at all. "Hi, Daddy," she said, kissing him.

"Why, honey," Grandpa said, seeming more flustered than she was, "I didn't expect you."

"You don't have an eightieth birthday every day."

"If I knew that was what it took to get you here, I'd have had one a lot sooner." He beamed at her. "You look beautiful, darling."

"I—" Mama looked like she was having trouble talking. She sat down next to him and took his hand. "How do you like Eliane?"

"I'm crazy about her," he said. "She's going to take me to Paris with her."

"We'd love to have you," Mama said. "Could you come?"

"I might if enough people begged me and somebody'd be around to plunk me on the plane." Then Grandpa noticed my cast. "Pretty impressive," he said. "Anybody got a pen?"

An old lady gave him one, and he signed his name real big, "Grandpa," in purple. Then Duff and Anita drew little animals and flowers all over it so it would be attractive, not just an ordinary cast.

"How much longer will you be staying around here?" Grandpa asked.

Mama told him we were flying back next week.

"Next time you better stay longer," he said. "Give this girl a chance to get to know us."

"She's going to stay for the whole summer next year," Duff told him. That was something we planned.

"That's more like it. A week or two isn't anything. Especially after all these years." He kept looking from Mama to me while he talked.

Then the nurse brought in the birthday cake Duff had made. She'd lit all the candles. It felt hot when you got close up, all those candles going at once. I offered to help Grandpa blow them out.

"I believe in lighting candles, not in blowing them out. I'm just going to let them die down naturally, the way I am." But once they did, he ate a great big piece of cake and seemed to like it. "I feel overfed and overstimulated," he said with satisfaction.

"Are we tiring you too much?" Anita wanted to know.

"No way. I like it. It's *too* quiet around this place. Cheating at cards is the only excitement I get." To Duff he said, "I miss our fishing trips. I need a little adventure now that I'm creeping up toward ninety."

He pushed away his plate. "Paris on my eighty-first birthday. I like that. Will you show me all the sights, Miss Ellie?"

"Sure," I said. "I could show you Nana's farm, too."

"Who's this Nana?"

"My French grandma."

"Well, I want to meet her, but nothing serious, tell her. I have a girl friend for every day of the week in this place. The ratio's just perfect." He winked at me. "It's a date, then. You'll remember? August eighteenth. Don't go making dates with any other fellows. Don't go fickle on me."

"I won't," I promised, and blushed.

Before we left I gave Grandpa a book I'd found in a store: *Teach Yourself French*. I thought if he was really coming to Paris, he ought to practice up. "Well, I never was too wonderful at languages," he said, opening it, "but this looks easy. . . . *Comment allez-vous?''* he read in a funny accent. "How are you?"

"That's good, Grandpa," I said, to be encouraging. But he better practice or no one'll know what he's saying.

"By the time I get there, I'll be so good those French people won't be able to keep up with me," he said.

The only trouble is he won't have anyone to practice *with*, but I can write him letters in French. I promised I would.

Chapter 20

We're back in Paris now. School's started again. Everything seems the same. But it isn't. I'm different. Jean-Claude said he could tell. He said I looked different than before I left, but when I asked him how, he said he couldn't explain it exactly. He asked if I'd looked up Peter while I was there, and I said yes but that we'd stayed over at his house only one day. "He has another girl friend," I said.

Jean-Claude looked pleased at that. "I figured he would."

This is terrible, but I think I might like someone else from school. He's from America too, and his name is Lance Schuman. He comes from Pennsylvania, not that far from where Duff and Anita live. He says he's even been in Swarthmore!

Well, I haven't made up my mind yet that he's going to be my boyfriend in any serious way. But he's good to talk to, and he seems to know how to kiss pretty well. Maybe not as good as Peter, but that's just because he never did it that much before. I'm his first girl friend, he says.

I told everyone at school about my having a brother—a half brother. I pretended that I'd known about it all along, just that I hadn't ever seen him before. Yvonne thought that was strange. "How come you never mentioned him?" she said.

I shrugged. Usually I tell her everything, but I didn't tell her everything about the summer. I didn't tell her about Mama's going off or about Nicholas. I don't feel like talking about that so much.

I wrote to Nicholas. He's in medical school and working really hard. He says he broke up with Tara. He and Anita are still in love with each other, but he says he just isn't sure what's going to happen next. "I'm taking things as they come," he wrote, "or trying to anyway."

Grandpa writes me too. He writes in English. In each letter he puts in a few French expressions. I wonder if he really will come over. Mama said she wasn't sure he'd be up to it and that I shouldn't count on it. I'm not, but I still hope he'll come. I told Nana about him, and she said she was looking forward to meeting him and that he could stay at her farm. She said she'd cook him good, nourishing meals and make him feel right at home. "He should be proud, reaching eighty," she said. I told her I thought he was.

Despite everything, I haven't forgiven Mama for going off. She says harboring grudges is bad and got her into lots of trouble and she hates to think I'm following in her footsteps in that regard. I'm not—I just don't feel she's ever given me a satisfactory explanation of why she acted like that. "Some things can't be explained," she'll say.

"Then they can't be forgiven either," I say back.

She says when I'm grown and have children of my own, I'll realize.

"Realize what?"

"That you can't be perfect all the time, that sometimes you reach the end of your rope."

I reach the end of my rope *lots* of times! What kind of excuse is that? But I still am glad to have her back. Sometimes I wake up in the middle of the night with a funny scared feeling, the kind I used to get when I was little. I'll get out of bed and creep into Mama's bedroom. Usually she's sleeping with her arm flung over her eyes and the white blanket falling half off the bed. She looks so peaceful sleeping I don't wake her up. I just sit there, thinking. I can't always fall right back to sleep. When I'm lying in bed, I think back to lots of things, staying over with Nicholas and Rae at that motel and catching Roe sneaking into my room to steal my bra. Sometimes I remember that feeling when I jumped off the roof, sailing out into the air, scared, wishing I hadn't done it and knowing it was going to hurt really bad when I came down.

My leg's all fine now and the cast is off. But I kept it because I like the drawings Anita and Duff made. I like Grandpa's signature all squiggly and purple going clear from one end of it to the other. It makes me remember everything that happened, even the bad parts.

My father used to say he wanted to photograph everything in life, all that he saw; he didn't want to screen anything out.

I think I know what he meant.